THE MISSING MAN

THE
MISSING
MAN

Hillary Waugh

PERENNIAL LIBRARY
Harper & Row, Publishers
New York, Cambridge, Philadelphia, San Francisco
London, Mexico City, São Paulo, Sydney

THE MISSING MAN. Copyright © 1964 by Hillary Waugh. All rights reserved. Printed
in the United States of America. No part of this book may be used or reproduced in
any manner whatsoever without written permission except in the case of brief
quotations embodied in critical articles and reviews. For information address
Doubleday & Co., Inc., 245 Park Avenue, New York, N.Y. 10016. Published
simultaneously in Canada by Fitzhenry & Whiteside Limited, Toronto.

First PERENNIAL LIBRARY edition published 1981.

ISBN: 0-06-080553-6

81 82 83 84 85 10 9 8 7 6 5 4 3 2 1

THE MISSING MAN

CHAPTER I

Jack Winthrop, barefoot and in bathing trunks, his "Lifeguard" sun helmet cocked on the back of his head, opened one of the many doors to the pavilion and padded across the empty dance floor towards the soda-fountain room. He was a curly-headed youth of husky build with a roll of well-tanned flesh bulging above the top of his trunks. In the vast space of the dance floor the atmosphere of last night's cigarettes and beer still lingered but the aroma of fresh coffee was stronger and Jack followed it to its source, yawning and blinking.

Morrie, a small wiry man of indeterminate age was sweeping the floor of the fountain room, getting the sand and bottle caps and bits of paper out from under the tables with quick, busy strokes. The clock over the counter said 7:35 in the morning but he looked as if he'd been awake for hours.

"Brother," Jack sighed, wincing at the bright beauty of lake scenery through the windows, "it's going to be another scorcher." He slumped onto a stool at the counter and propped his head with his hand.

Morrie leaned the broom against the wall and got the youth a cup of coffee from the large urn that bubbled merrily behind the counter. He took a tiny bottle of milk from the icebox and set it beside the cup, then pushed the sugar bowl over. "Last weekend of the season," he said, "and then it's back to school, huh?"

"Yeah," Jack answered and picked a piece of sunburned skin from the tip of his nose. "Back to rest up from the summer. God, what a rat-race."

"So," said Morrie, "I see you dancing with all the pretty girls every night. You know you gotta get up in the morning."

Jack dumped two spoonfuls of sugar into the coffee without unpropping himself and stirred. "What do you think I'm going to do when I get through lifeguarding, go to bed?"

Morrie said, "I would, but then I ain't young like you no more. I ain't got your stamina."

He went back to his broom and Jack lethargically dumped the milk into his coffee and started to sip. "Besides," he said, "who can sleep on those sandbag mattresses those tourist homes give you? How the hell can you stand it living in Little Bohemia?"

"It's a nice place," Morrie said, reaching under another table. "We got a big house, a nice view of the lake."

"They're all big and they're all falling on each other," the boy complained. "Ramshackle houses that feel like ovens; narrow streets you can't park on; narrow sidewalks; a bunch of beatniks who think they're artists. You have to drive two miles to Stockford if you want anything more than a pack of cigarettes or loaf of bread and then, in the summertime, every house packs in tourists till they spill into the water. Brother!"

Morrie laughed. "That dame you were with last night must've given you a hard time."

"A bag," Jack said. "Strictly a bag. One of those beatnik artist neighbors of yours. If she can paint I can fly. Little Bohemia! That's the name for that little spit of land of yours all right. Put three houses on it and it'd be all right but because it sticks out at the end of the lake they put sixty houses on it and everybody moves in."

Another youth in lifeguard helmet and trunks appeared in the doorway. He was dark and slender and in a sunnier mood. "Hi, Morrie," he said and went to Jack, clapping him on the shoulder. "How'd you make out with that broad last night? She didn't look too bad."

"A beast," Jack told him. "I wouldn't touch her with gloves."

Morrie got the newcomer some coffee and said, "Don't mind him, Butch. He's sorry to see the end of summer come."

"Sure," Butch said. "It's a tough life. Sit in the sun all day and flirt with pretty girls in bathing suits."

"And clean up the beach," Morrie reminded him. "Where's Gary? You guys better get at it. It's supposed to be all neat and tidy by nine o'clock and there was a big mob here yesterday."

Jack got off his stool and drained his cup. "Yeah," he said. "Two more days of cleaning detail and then it's over. Tomorrow night I'm going to get stinko." He went to a small closet and got out a burlap sack, a rake and a sharp, metal-tipped stick.

Butch said to Morrie, "I guess that girl must've given him a knife last night."

Gary, the third lifeguard, came in then, yawning. "God," he said. "You drag yourself out of bed like it's the middle of the night and you come out and there's blazing sunshine all over the place like you ought to've been up hours ago."

"What time did you get to bed?" Butch asked him.

"Three o'clock." He took a stool for his cup of Morrie's coffee.

Jack carried his equipment to the door and looked out at the quarter mile of beach the three of them had to clean up before nine o'clock. Even from the pavilion the discarded bottles and papers were visible. As if there weren't enough trash cans around! "I'll start at the far end," he told the others, "and work down. You two work up."

He went out and down the veranda steps to the sand. To his left the horde of shingled houses known as Little Bohemia gleamed in the morning sun against a bright blue September sky. To his right stretched the glare of beach, damp from the dew and still cool from the night air. Across the lake a background of blue-gray pines spiked the sky while here and there a cabin and boatdock caught the sun. It was the last Sunday of summer and it promised to finish the season in style.

To Jack there was no beauty in the view. The orange, slanted rays of sun painted it with distaste for the early light was an always familiar reminder of the too little sleep of the night before and the too many hours of the day ahead. He prepared himself to endure and started his chores, turning his back on Little Bohemia and starting up the long stretch of beach, keeping to the back where the overhang of grass and trees formed little nooks and crannies.

He plodded slowly, the sack and rake dragging a trail behind him, and he kept his eyes open. The beach was a hot necking spot after dark, especially in the little hollows, and he wanted to catch any evidences the lovers left behind before the children came around. Jack was fond of children and he wanted to keep them protected.

His tour of the irregular edge of beach was uneventful throughout the main portion but, some eighty yards short of the far end, something so unexpected caught his eye that it brought him to a dead and open-mouthed stop. Up ahead, projecting from a nook, were a pair of bare feet.

Jack stared at them and blinked but they didn't go away. He started forward again carefully, detouring farther onto the beach and coming around. He coughed a little to give their owner warning but there was no movement.

The feet belonged to a girl, he found as he came into view. She was lying quietly on her back with her hands at her side, high heeled pumps close by. The skirt of her frock was mussed a little, showing an inch of left thigh and a bit of pretty, ruffled slip. She was a young, dark-haired girl with trim, well-shaped legs, an attractively-developed figure and a face that should have been really beautiful except something seemed to be wrong with it.

Jack came closer, sensing that she wasn't asleep but not sure just what was the matter with her and why she was there. It wasn't till he got very close that he saw. Around her throat was a necklace that was not a necklace. It was a piece of heavy cord and it was knotted so tightly that it bit into the flesh.

Jack had a momentary urge to get that cord off quickly so she could breathe and he even made a move towards her before it dawned on him that the cord had been there far too long and she hadn't drawn a breath in too many hours for it to make any difference any more.

Jack Winthrop had never seen a dead person before, not even in a coffin, and he stared at this one in disbelief. Her purplish face was slightly bloated and the rest of her flesh was waxy white but she looked so real that it took a good half minute for him to get it into his head that she wouldn't at any moment open her eyes, smile at him and get up.

Eventually comprehension came through and he took a step back, appalled and slightly sick. A beautiful girl like that, a girl you could get mellow about just thinking of holding her in your arms, and someone had choked her to death.

He shook himself and at last got free of the numbing effects of shock. Then he turned and sprinted back the way he had come.

CHAPTER II

The call came into police headquarters in the basement of the Stockford Town Hall at ten after eight that Sunday morning. The patrols had gone out and Chief of Police Fred C. Fellows and Sergeant T. C. Unger were having a cup of coffee at the main desk. Unger picked up the phone and said into it with his usual, noncommittal voice, "Police Department, Sergeant Unger." It was a tone that was supposed to convey to excited callers a sense of the world still turning, of life still going on, so it can't be as bad as all that.

It had no such effect on young Jack Winthrop in his booth at the pavilion with two other startled lifeguards and a nervous Morrie gathered outside. "Police?" he said frantically. "There's a dead girl on the beach!"

Unger frowned but kept his voice modulated. "There's a dead girl where?"

"On the beach. At Indian Lake. She's dead!"

"She drowned, you mean?"

"No, no, not drowned. Strangled. She's been strangled!"

"Strangled?" Unger was losing his own aplomb. "You mean murdered?"

At those words Fellows snapped his fingers imperatively and Unger passed him the phone. "This is Chief Fellows," he said into it. "Who's this speaking?"

The youth had to think. "Uh—my name is Jack Winthrop. I'm a lifeguard at Indian Lake. I just found a dead girl on the beach!"

"All right," the chief said, calming his voice. "Don't get excited. Let's have it slowly. You say the girl's dead? Are you sure of that?"

"What? Yes. Of course I'm sure. She's lying on the sand and she's dead."

"Whereabouts is this?"

"Up at the end of the beach. I found her. I was cleaning the beach and there she was with a rope around her neck, dead. She's been strangled or something and her face is all purple and she's just lying there."

"There's a rope around her neck?"

"Well, like a piece of cord, tied very tight. I don't know how long she's been there but she looks like she's made of wax and she looks stiff and cold."

"You touch her?" Fellows asked.

"No, sir. Not me."

"All right, I'll tell you what you do. Go back where she is and don't let anybody near her, not within twenty feet and that means you too. Wait for us there. We'll be right out. You understand that?"

"Yes, sir. But I'm supposed to help clean up the beach. Should I—"

"Never mind the beach. You stand guard where the body is till we get there. Jack Winthrop you say your name is?"

"Yes. I'm a lifeguard at the beach."

"Wait for us."

Fellows put down the phone and stared at Unger. "It looks

like a murder, all right," he said, "if that kid knows what he's talking about."

"At Indian Lake beach? At a resort?"

"That's what he says and it doesn't sound like a gag." Fellows shrugged. "Well, there goes Wilks' Labor Day weekend. Better call him up, T.C., and get him out there. Get hold of Hank Lemmon and tell him to bring his camera. If you can't reach him, tell Lewis to bring *his* camera. I'll want him there with his notebook anyway. Then get MacFarlane and tell him he'll need an ambulance. After that you'd better let Clem Avery know in case he wants to have a look. You got all that?"

"Yes," Unger said, writing. "You're sure it's not a prank? I mean—on the beach?"

"If it is there's going to be hell to pay because we've got to play it for real." Fellows went to the bulletin board. "I'll want four supers," he said and ran his finger down the list. "Pebble, Sokoloff, Kovacks and I guess McDonnell." He returned and picked up the mike. "Car one, car two."

"Car one," came over the receiving set from Patrolman Joseph Dzanowski. "Car two, go ahead," followed immediately from Zolton Chernoff.

"There's a body reported on the beach at Indian Lake," Fellows announced. "Pick up Cassidy and Raphael and get out there. It's at the north end with a lifeguard named Jack Winthrop standing by."

The cars acknowledged and Fellows said to Unger, "Call up Harris and Lambert. They're to take over Cassidy's and Raphael's assignments." He made for the door with his big strides and went out to his battered gray coupe.

Indian Lake was south of town, out Lake Avenue, and the only public road to it was the one to Little Bohemia at the south end, half a mile below High Ridge Road. Fellows made the better than two-mile run with his siren shrieking and pulled into the vast acres of nearly deserted public parking lot back of the pavilion in just under three minutes. When he got out and his own siren faded, the approaching wails of two others could be heard against the bright, glittering sky.

The lifeguards, Butch and Gary, came out of the pavilion with Morrie the moment the chief's car stopped and he strode towards them saying, "You know about this body supposed to be on the beach?"

They nodded and Butch pointed. "She's way up there at that end. Jack's guarding her."

"Jack the one who found her?"

Butch said, "Yes. We went up and took a look but came back to direct you."

"You know who she is?"

There were shaking heads and assurances that they'd never seen her before.

Fellows pulled out his notebook and asked a few questions. The lifeguards were named Henry Buckley and Gary Stone. They and Jack all had rooms in a Mrs. Walker's tourist home on Number Two Street in adjacent Little Bohemia. Morrie's name was Leibman and he and his family had a house on Lakeside Street, the main road. He'd lived there twenty years, working in the pavilion summers and down in Florida winters. The lifeguards had been hired from June 15 through Labor Day and neither had worked the lake before.

Fellows took their home addresses and turned as the two squad cars arrived almost simultaneously and disgorged their four occupants. He told the youths that more reinforcements would be arriving and asked them to point the way. To the policemen he said, "Well, let's go see what there is to see," and started for the nearest ramp to the beach.

CHAPTER III

Jack Winthrop was visible way up the beach pacing the sand down around the water's edge when Fellows, with Dzanowski, Chernoff, Cassidy and Raphael in tow, came off the ramp. The policemen plodded their way over the long stretch of soft sand and Jack came forward to meet them. "I didn't touch a thing," he said. "Nobody's come around."

Fellows let him lead them to the spot, gestured the boy and the others back and went forward himself for a close look. He stared at the girl for a bit, noting her youth and her beauty as well as her position, the wrinkles in her skirt, her clenched hands, the ugly tight cord cutting into her throat. He shook his head soberly, then bent to study the sand around her body, stepping carefully. "These marks made by your feet, son?" he asked Jack, gesturing.

"These over here are mine where I was coming up on her. I didn't make those there."

Fellows nodded and worked out farther away. He stooped suddenly and picked up a cigarette butt stuck in the sand. "Filter tip," he said, holding it for scrutiny. "It's not yours, is it?"

Jack swallowed. "I'm afraid it is."

"You leave it here last night or this morning?"

"Just now. I smoked it while I was waiting."

Fellows handed it to him. "Take care of it, will you? I wouldn't like it to get mixed up with legitimate clues. Anything else of yours around here? A match for the cigarette?"

"No, sir. I used a lighter. I'm sorry. I didn't think."

"Don't worry about it. We caught it in time." He turned and regarded the body again. "Sand on her feet," he said. "She

walked and carried the shoes. No purse. That's too bad. You
didn't happen to notice a purse did you, son?"

Jack shook his head. "There was nothing, sir. Just the shoes."

Fellows went off again, detouring well around the nook where
the girl lay, and climbed the small embankment to examine the
grass and bushes above. It would have been difficult for the girl
to have come to the beach from there and she would have left
signs. Fellows found none and returned again.

The other four policemen still stood as a group, watching in
silence, and when Fellows took out his chewing tobacco and bit
off a piece, Jack said, "Aren't you going to do anything?"

Fellows replaced the tobacco packet in his shirt pocket. "Such
as what?"

"Examine her or something?"

"Not till we get photographs taken. I've been meaning to ask
you, by the way. Have you ever seen this girl before?"

Jack shook his head. "No, sir."

"No idea where she comes from or where she might live?"

"No, sir."

"What were you doing last night after dark?"

Jack looked suddenly frightened. "Me?"

Fellows smiled at him. "I'm not suggesting you had anything
to do with this, son. I'm trying to get the lay of the land around
here. If she came out on the beach with some man she might
have been inside dancing in the pavilion earlier. I'm just wondering if you happened to be around the pavilion last night."

"Yes, sir. I was. But I had a date."

"You were dancing?"

"Yes, sir."

"Did you come down on the beach?"

"No, we didn't."

"Not even for a minute to look at the moon? It's almost a full
moon right now."

"No, sir. We didn't come onto the beach at all."

"You've had time enough to look at her and think about it
but you're still sure you didn't see her inside the pavilion last
night?"

"Yes, sir. I'm sure."

"Let's put it this way. If you had seen her do you think you'd remember?"

Jack nodded. "I think so. She looks as if she'd been very beautiful and I think I'd remember the dress."

Detective Sergeant Sidney G. Wilks appeared on the beach in the distance and Fellows, marking time, said, "I wish it was Lemmon, damn it, so we could get those pictures out of the way." He queried the boy then as to his home address and asked about his job and how he and the other lifeguards spent their time. Jack told him they were due to show up at half past seven every morning to clean up the beach. Thereafter, from nine until seven in the evening they worked lifeguard duty in shifts, four on, two off. After seven their time was their own.

Wilks came up to the group as Jack was explaining that one of the boys had a car but since Stockford was a pretty dead town they usually spent their evenings hanging around the pavilion at night. Fellows jotted a few words on his pad and then greeted the detective sergeant. "Sorry to disturb your weekend, Sid. I hope you didn't have plans."

"A policeman have plans? Funny man." He stepped forward past the chief for his first look at the body and then went around and closer as Fellows had done. Fellows said, "Don't go spoil those footprints."

"Footprints?" Wilks gave a short laugh. "If you think you could get any footprints out of this soft sand you're a magician. Where's her purse?"

"There isn't any purse."

"I'll bet there used to be." Wilks stood over the dead girl with his hands on his hips and studied her. "Lipstick's smudged," he said. "No rings. No jewelry. No stockings. What's the guess on no pants?"

"We're going to wait a while before we go after the answer to that one."

"Twenty-two years old. Twenty-three at the most. She's a beautiful thing too, poor kid." He came back and shook his head. "That's going to be tough news for some mother and father.

Any calls come in from parents whose daughter didn't get home last night?"

"Not as of ten after eight this morning."

"Which means she doesn't come from around here or her parents went to bed before she was due in and haven't waked up yet." He nodded at Jack Winthrop. "This the boy who found her?"

Jack said he was and added, "I—uh—don't know if you know but a lot of necking goes on here. They—ah—go pretty far sometimes. Ah—even all the way."

"We know," Fellows said. "This place is rather notorious. In fact, from what I hear, a girl shows she's willing to play it hot and heavy just by coming down on this beach with a boy." He turned and regarded the body for a moment. "I wonder," he said thoughtfully, "if this one maybe didn't know about that?"

Dzanowski spoke up angrily. "It ain't no good. We ought to patrol this beach."

"If we had the men," Fellows answered sadly. "But what's the difference, Joe? They'd just go someplace else. Anybody who'd do it on the beach with other couples around is going to do it, period. You aren't going to stop them."

Dzanowski still glowered. "I don't care. Whoever do it to that little girl there—" He made a wrenching motion with his fists. "I break his neck."

CHAPTER IV

By the time Hank Lemmon, photographer for the *Stockford Weekly Bulletin*, arrived with his camera, the first of the beach enthusiasts were appearing and Fellows dispatched Dzanowski to keep them back. Dzanowski, still grim, did it thoroughly. He wouldn't let anyone within fifty yards of the police.

Lemmon took half a dozen pictures from varying angles and Fellows, having no further use for Jack Winthrop, sent the youth back to his own work. "I guess the beach won't get a cleaning to-day," he said, "but you've done your job already. I'm much obliged."

Three more policemen arrived as Lemmon was finishing up, plainclothesman Edward N. Lewis and supernumeraries Pebble and McDonnell. They joined the swelling group of officers watching Lemmon and waiting for orders.

Lemmon put his camera back in the bag with the flashbulbs and film plates and said, "I'll have these ready by noon, Fred. Five by sevens big enough?"

"I'd rather have eight by tens. Glossy, of course."

The photographer nodded and started off. Fellows turned then to his men. "All right, let's start to work. McDonnell, we're going to have to sift this sand. You work for a contractor, don't you? You think your boss will let us borrow three, make it four shovels and a screen? Go pick them up, will you? Pebble, you go with him. Chernoff, you, Cassidy and Raphael, we don't have an identification yet. You can start on that. Begin with Little Bohemia. Go up and take a good close look at the girl's face and her dress. Then get over there and make inquiries."

The men went up to the body and gathered around it for a close study, then started off. Fellows watched them go and looked on up the beach. "I don't know when MacFarlane's go-ing to get here," he said, turning back, "but time's awasting. Let's see what the story is on her pants, Sid."

He approached the body again with Wilks, took the girl's an-kles and raised her legs. The body was stiff and her hips came free of the sand so that Wilks could slide her pretty print dress and ruffled slip over them. He pushed up the skirt and slip clum-sily, then took hold on both sides and stripped them back to her waist.

Fellows lowered her feet again. "No pants," he said without surprise. He knelt beside her, bending close, and ran a brief finger over the top of her leg where it met the torso. "No marks." He grasped the bunched clothing at her waist and yanked it higher. A faint, straight puckered line ran across her flesh and Fellows traced that with his finger. "There it is," he said. "She had pants on when she came here. I guess the boy took them with him."

Wilks observed the indication and nodded. Fellows let go of the dress. "She didn't have them off too long before she was killed or the elastic mark would have faded."

"I guess she said no and meant it," Wilks said. "Granny knot in that cord around her neck. The guy tied it tight."

Fellows bent close over the girl's clenched left hand. "She wore a ring, Sid," he said. "Fourth finger left hand."

"Wedding? That could be the story right there."

"Or engagement," Fellows said. "Or a school ring." He got to his feet slowly and looked down at her face. "She's a pretty girl, Sid. Without any pants it looks like sex and MacFarlane will tell us if that's right or not. Without any ring, though, and without any purse, that looks like robbery. The two don't go together."

Wilks got up too. "I'd say sex, Fred. If the purse is missing it's to keep us from identifying her."

Fellows shook his head. "I don't know. That doesn't account for the missing ring and there shouldn't be any trouble identifying her, purse or no purse." He shrugged. "Well, I guess it doesn't matter to her any more but we might as well have some modesty around here. Help me get her skirt down again."

Wilks obliged, pulling it back into place while the chief held her legs. When they were finished the skirt was about where it had been but slightly more mussed. Fellows studied the result and said, "It was wrinkled like that before. I'll bet that's what the boy did after he strangled her, pulled her skirt back down."

The other two supernumeraries had arrived and now the medical examiner, Dr. James MacFarlane, white-haired and slow of foot was coming up the beach with two ambulance attendants and a stretcher. The crowd of bathers had grown but few were bathing. Most were clustered as close as Dzanowski would let them come, whispering and watching with the solemnity that death imposes.

MacFarlane gave a brief greeting to Fellows and Wilks and went directly to the body, kneeling beside it for examination. Carleton Lawrence, the editor of the *Stockford Weekly Bulletin*, joined the group, Fellows telling Dzanowski to let him through. "I stopped off at headquarters," he said. "Just in case there were any reports I should bring you."

"Unger didn't say anything about a call from worried parents, did he?"

"No."

"That's something of a problem." Fellows looked at his watch. "Nine o'clock. If a girl were missing it should have been discovered by now."

"No identification?"

"Not yet." Fellows turned to regard the group of curious bathers and rubbed his chin. "It's a funny way to go about things, Sid," he said to Wilks, "but maybe we should let them have a look. One of them might know her."

"It won't hurt, I guess. I'll go talk to them."

MacFarlane completed his preliminary examination and climbed slowly to his feet, brushing the sand from his trouser knees. "I'd estimate death occurred nine to eleven hours ago, Fred. Cause is almost certainly strangulation. No marks or bruises on the part of her that's visible. I'll know more after an autopsy, of course."

Fellows nodded. "Between ten last night and midnight. There was a good moon last night too. It would've been pretty light on the beach. That would make it probably closer to twelve than ten. Fewer people around. Even so, the guy must have been desperate to kill her in a place like this in the moonlight."

"You're sure she was killed here and not dumped?"

"She wasn't dragged. That much is certain. I won't swear she couldn't have been carried. The sand's too soft to measure depth of footprints or anything like that but it's not likely she was carried. That would mean waiting till the beach was empty of people and if it was empty, why carry her the whole length of it? Besides, her feet are sandy. She walked in sand *someplace*."

"You're probably right. Is there anything else you want to do or shall I take her?"

"You can take her. But check with Wilks on your way out. We'd like to show her to those people back there and anyone else who wants a look. She didn't drop out of the sky and somebody might have seen her."

MacFarlane beckoned to the two white-jacketed men with the stretcher. It was opened and ready and they brought it forward and laid it beside the girl. All of the policemen came forward as if it were a ceremony and watched the two attendants lift the dead girl whose pretty features they would never see again, position her on the stretcher, tuck in her shoes, and cover her over with a clean sheet. When they raised her makeshift bier, Fellows said, "Keep her face exposed, Doc, and enough of her dress to show what it's like."

MacFarlane made the adjustments and started off after the attendants, plodding as if he carried the weight of the world on his shoulders and was wearied. They stopped to show the girl to the fifteen or so curious watchers but there was no recognition. MacFarlane covered the girl again and started on.

McDonnell and Pebble passed him coming back with four shovels and the sand sieve borrowed from the Blake Co., Contractors. Fellows turned to the nook which now seemed strangely empty yet still not normal. There was a forlorn quality to the mussed sand where the girl had lain. The indentations were the last impressions she had made upon the earth, the last thing she had done, but her final marks were to be of short duration.

Fellows gestured at the spot. "Start digging," he said.

CHAPTER V

Four supernumeraries shoveled sand till eleven o'clock and it was hot work under the climbing sun. The project was a large one, for Fellows made them sift the top layer of beach over as wide an area as he could stretch with reasonable assurance that anything found might belong either to the girl or to her killer.

Nothing was uncovered, however—not so much as a match, let alone the missing ring from her fourth finger left hand. As shovelful after shovelful of sand was thrown against the screen the only objects that accumulated were shells.

The job was just finishing when the first break in the case came. Patrolman Zolton Chernoff in the company of a plump, gray-haired man strode up the beach as Fellows and the supernumeraries were quitting the scene. "I got something," he said. "I think I got a lead. Tell him, Mr. Ecklund."

The gray-haired man said, "I'm a photographer. I think I took a picture of the girl. Same dress from what the officer says. Beige with a brown and orange abstract design? Good quality dress? Dark-haired girl with lovely bone construction, beautiful features?"

"That's right," the chief said. "And you photographed her?"

He nodded. "She came into my studio Friday to have her picture taken. I took six. She was to come in for the proofs on Tuesday."

"Are the proofs ready now?"

"Right in my studio. You want me to show them to you?"

"I'd be obliged if you would."

They went back to the ramp by the parking area and Wilks and Dzanowski joined them from the pavilion. "Haven't found anybody yet who knows her," Wilks said, "and I just checked with Unger on the car radio. He still hasn't got any missing persons calls. I don't think the girl's from around here."

"She may live in Little Bohemia," Fellows told him. "It's starting to look that way."

The supernumeraries were sent back with the sifting equipment and Fellows, Wilks, Dzanowski and Chernoff accompanied the photographer around the pavilion to the narrow street that ran out onto the peninsula through the thick cluster of houses.

The studio was on the main street, one flight up in a shingled building. A wooden sign nailed beside the door said, "Joseph Ecklund, Photographer" and in a glass case in the hall were samples of his art.

He brought them through a door at the top of the stairs into the reek of developer. It spread from his dark rooms at the back through the dingy passage and into the narrow sitting room that overlooked the junction of Lakeside and Number Four Street. A few props were there, screens, chairs, a large portrait camera and metal lamps on six-foot stands.

Fellows crossed the faded carpet and looked out of the low-silled window down the short stretch of Number Four Street to Indian River where it cut around Little Bohemia on leaving the lake. A surprising number of people were in sight, most on foot with a few on bikes. No cars were around for there was no parking on the tiny streets and no room between houses for driveways. Cars could only come in and go out, which made it pointless for any but sightseers.

Mr. Ecklund came briskly out of his back room with the half dozen proofs in his hand. "These are the ones," he said, handing them to the chief. "Now, is that the young lady?"

On top was a picture of a dark-haired girl shown from the waist up, full face, with a slight and very nice smile. "Yes," Fellows said, nodding. "She's the one."

"A lovely thing. So very photogenic. Is that the same dress?"

"The same dress too," Fellows told him. He showed the picture to Wilks and passed it to the others.

The second picture showed the girl resting her chin against

her left hand and Wilks said instantly, "It's a wedding ring! What do you know about that?"

"And a watch," Fellows said. "She's wearing a wristwatch."

"That's right," Ecklund put in. "It was a very lovely watch. Diamond studded."

Fellows held the picture closer. "I count ten tiny diamonds around that crystal. Is that what you get, Sid?"

"Ten," Wilks said. "You don't need glasses yet."

"Chips or cut diamonds? Can you tell?"

"It's cut diamonds," Ecklund put in. "It was a very expensive watch."

Fellows said, "Her wedding ring, her wristwatch and her purse, Sid. And she's from around here. That wasn't to hide her identity. That was robbery."

"He robbed her of her pants too, don't forget, and I don't think there's much monetary value in women's underpants."

Fellows passed on to the next picture and the ones after. They were good poses and showed Ecklund's ability but there was nothing further to be learned from them. Fellows handed them on and said to Ecklund, "What's the girl's name and address?"

Ecklund, who'd been looking pleased with himself, lost his smile. "Well, I don't know."

"She didn't leave a name? You didn't request a name?"

"Well, no. She walked in in the middle of Friday afternoon, along about four o'clock I'd say, and told me she'd seen my sign and wanted her picture taken. So I sat her down and posed her and said I'd have the proofs ready Tuesday and she said she'd drop in Tuesday afternoon. She didn't leave a name and I didn't ask her for one."

"Some way to do business," Fellows growled.

"Well I didn't know she was going to get killed," Ecklund said defensively. "Anyhow, I'm sure she lives here. Practically no one comes from anywhere else to have me take their picture."

Fellows collected the proofs from his men and straightened them. "All right, Mr. Ecklund. This helps a lot anyway. I'll just

take these along if you don't mind. Also, may I have the negatives?"

"For which poses?"

"All of them."

Ecklund wet his lips. "It costs me money. She hired me and—"

"We'll pay you for them," Fellows said a little shortly. "Send a
bill to the police department."

Ecklund accepted that and brought out the negatives and two
envelopes. Fellows thanked him, turned the negatives over to
Wilks for prints and kept the proofs himself. "All right, Dzanowski, I want you and Chernoff to get busy on these houses here.
Team up with Raphael and Cassidy and do a door to door canvass. It's almost certain that girl lived around here and I want to
know where it was and who she is." He started for the door with
Wilks.

CHAPTER VI

Hank Lemmon's photographs of the body came into headquarters at noon as promised and Fellows looked them over while
eating his lunch of a ham sandwich and thermos of coffee. He
studied the way she was lying, the wrinkles in her skirt, the way
her hands were clenched, the position of the cord around her
throat, but he couldn't come up with any meanings he hadn't
considered before.

Sid Wilks came into the office at quarter past twelve and
sorted through the pictures too. "Nothing significant that I can
see," he said, slipping them back into the envelope.

Fellows tossed the envelope onto his cluttered rolltop desk
and looked up at the pictures of nude girls that adorned the

wall above. "Sex?" he asked soberly, regarding them. "A raven-haired beauty with a luscious figure and a pair of missing pants. She's found in a spot that's only used for necking. It's almost got to be sex."

Wilks sat back. "That's the obvious answer. You certainly wouldn't deliberately take a girl there to kill her. That makes the killing a sudden act of passion when she wouldn't give in."

Fellows swung his chair around slowly. "That's right," he said. "All very neat and tidy except for a few odds and ends."

"It's sex, Fred. No guy would take a girl down there on the beach to steal her wristwatch either. Nor would he have to kill her to get it."

"That's not the loose end I was thinking about. You know the story of the slave who did *not* get to marry the Pharaoh's daughter?"

"The *what?*"

"Well, back in old Egypt," Fellows went on, "there was once a very ambitious slave and he thought if he could win the hand of his master's daughter he'd get to rule the kingdom because his master happened to be the Pharaoh himself. He worked long and hard at always being at the right spot at the right time and anticipating the Pharaoh's every need. He got so good at it that no matter what the Pharaoh desired, the slave would promptly produce it and say, 'Oh, gracious Pharaoh, I just happened to have it on me.'

"This made him the most trusted and faithful slave of the Pharaoh but it didn't win him the daughter's hand so the ambitious slave went a step further. He arranged with confederates so that when he and the Pharaoh and the Pharaoh's daughter were out riding their camels one day, the three of them were seized by the confederates, who were dressed like robbers, and locked in a deep, dark dungeon.

"The Pharaoh despaired of his life and said, 'O slave, if you can get us out of this predicament you may have anything you ask.' The slave asked if he might have the daughter's hand and to this request the Pharaoh readily acceded.

"Thereupon, the slave promptly produced a key and unlocked

the door of the dungeon and when the Pharaoh, in astonish-
ment, asked where he had come by such a key, the slave replied,
'Oh gracious Pharaoh, I just happened to have it on me.'

"Well, the sad ending of the story is that the slave didn't get
to marry the Pharaoh's daughter after all. The Pharaoh had him
put to death instead."

Wilks made a wry face. "All right," he said, "which one just
happened to have what on them last night?"

"The boy just happened to have on him, last night, a length
of cord exactly right for garroting a girl. So, in the extremity
of this frustration you talk about, when she denies him her
body, he produces this cord he *happens* to have and strangles
her with it. Most men in such a frenzy wouldn't even think of
the cord if they did have one. They'd throttle her with their
bare hands."

Wilks compressed his lips. "So you think it's robbery? He takes
her to a place where she'd be heard if she cried out and then
strangles her so she won't cry out because he wants her wristwatch and wedding ring?"

"And purse. We don't know what she had in her purse."

"Fill it with diamonds if you want. You still aren't going to
take a girl to a public place to rob her."

"I'm not saying he did. What bothers me is the cord. The
presence of the cord makes it look premeditated. But if the murder *was* premeditated, what kind of a cool character is it who
would do it on the beach with other couples necking nearby?"
Fellows mulled it over while he poured two cups of coffee and
handed one to Wilks. "Maybe the key lies in the wedding ring,"
he said. "What was her husband doing last night? That's the
thing to find out."

"The more pressing problem," Wilks retorted, "is first to find
out who she is."

Fellows shrugged. "I don't think that'll be too hard. The
more interesting problem to me is why nobody's reported her
missing."

They abandoned the problem while they had their coffee and
talked of other things. Both men knew it was fruitless to specu-

late on so little data. Later, when more of the blanks were filled in, they could expect to find the way pointed out to them.

A woman who could fill in some of the blanks was brought in by Cassidy as the chief and Wilks were putting aside the coffee. Her name was Mrs. William Fremont and she was a short, plump, aging woman who had never been in a police station before and she looked around nervously as if afraid she'd be clapped in a cell. "She runs a tourist home in Little Bohemia," Cassidy explained to the chief. "She thinks the dead girl was staying at her house."

Fellows smiled at the woman reassuringly, aware that his and Wilks' large proportions were overwhelming the little woman. "We appreciate your coming," he said. "The girl was renting a room?"

Mrs. Fremont nodded and found her voice. "Mrs. Moore," she blurted out. "Mrs. Elizabeth Moore. Arrived Friday week."

"That's the name of the dead girl?"

She grew suddenly uncertain. "Well, I—. When I heard about the kind of dress she was wearing, well I just assumed—"

Cassidy said, "Mrs. Moore had a similar dress. We went to her room but Mrs. Moore wasn't there."

Fellows told Mrs. Fremont that sounded important. He invited her into the office and gave her a seat at the table. Wilks followed and closed the door while Fellows hunted for the proofs on his cluttered desk. "Take a look at these, Mrs. Fremont," he said, pulling them from the envelope. "Do you recognize the girl?"

She stared at the top one for a moment, wordless, and her eyes filled with tears. "Oh, yes," she said softly. "Oh, it's her." She put the pictures down and fumbled in an overlarge purse for a handkerchief. Wilks produced one of his and she nodded her thanks while dabbing her eyes under her glasses. "It's so sad," she said. "That awful man."

Fellows gathered up the pictures and slipped them back into their envelope. "What man is that?"

"I don't know his name."

"What does he look like?"

Mrs. Fremont blew her nose gently and gave back the hand-kerchief. "I don't know that either," she said apologetically. "I never saw him."

Fellows swung his chair around and pulled in at the table, getting out his notebook. "I guess I'd understand this best if we start at the beginning. Would you tell us everything you can about Mrs. Moore?"

The nude calendar girls on the wall above the chief's desk caught Mrs. Fremont's eye. She started slightly and looked away, then drew herself up a little straighter and faced the chief once more. "Mrs. Moore?" she said. Her gaze wandered again and she pulled it back and tried to concentrate. "Let me see."

"How did she come to rent the room?" Fellows asked to start her off.

Mrs. Fremont did a little better then. "It was Friday, the twenty-third of August. That's the date. Middle of the after-noon. There was the doorbell and there was Betty." She went on to describe the first meeting. Betty had arrived wearing a blue linen suit and carrying a small suitcase. She was an attractive girl but quiet and with a tendency to be withdrawn. She had seen the vacancy sign outside and wanted a room for an indefinite period.

"She didn't engage the room in advance then?" Fellows asked, looking up from his notes.

"No. She just appeared. Out of the blue, like."

"Where is she from? Where's her home?"

"She didn't have any."

"Didn't she give an address when she registered?"

Mrs. Fremont shook her head. "I asked and she said she could put down Chicago if I insisted but she hadn't lived there for years. I got it that my place was going to be her home from now on and I wasn't going to be fussy about it. I require payment in advance, you know, so it wasn't that she could run out on me and I had the rooms going to waste. I just had her sign her name."

"She once lived in Chicago but you don't know where she last lived, is that right?"

"I think it was Pittsfield but I don't know where."

"How did she get to your house? Did she have a car?"

"No. No car. It was a bus she said she took. The one down Lake Avenue from the center here."

"If she came down from Pittsfield she'd have to change to a local bus there all right." Fellows turned, "Sid, tell Unger to get after that. I want to know if the local driver remembers her and then we can check the Pittsfield bus."

Wilks went out and Fellows went on, "Now let's get back to the business of the room. You say she didn't reserve a room in advance. Were there any inquiries about vacancies?"

"No. I said no."

"No woman—or man—called up a day or two before she came to find out if you had rooms?"

"Nobody."

"So, in other words, she comes by bus to your doorstep without knowing whether you'll have a room available or not?"

"That's not so surprising," Mrs. Fremont said. "Anybody who knows anything about the place knows there's always plenty of vacancies through the week. If I'd been full up there would have been other places that weren't."

"She knew what it was like there then?"

Mrs. Fremont was gaining confidence. She shrugged and said, "I suppose so. I didn't really ask her about where she heard of us."

Wilks slipped back into the office and leaned against the door. Fellows glanced at him and nodded. He studied his notes. "All right, she arrived on your doorstep on August twenty-third wanting to rent a room. Go on, please."

"I gave her one. Second floor back. Not the most expensive room but a nice one. Her clothes were quality but I somehow had the feeling, her being alone and all, that she might be having to go careful."

"And that's the room she took?"

Mrs. Fremont nodded. She glanced once at the calendar girls and thereafter ignored them. She was beginning to appreciate her importance. "Of course it was room and board," she said. "We serve meals. There were, I guess, eight of us in the house including me and we all eat together, the guests and myself. She was very quiet at first, very sober, and you couldn't get a thing out of her. All you'd get was 'yes' and 'no' and 'please' and 'thank you'. The rest of us didn't want to pry or make her unhappy with a lot of questions so we didn't force ourselves on her."

"Eight altogether, you say? That would be six other guests. Are they still there?"

"No. Some went. Right now, though, I got nineteen. That's including Betty. I'm full up for Labor Day."

"And what did Betty do while she was with you?"

"Most of the time she stayed in her room. Other times she'd go out. She was out most every afternoon and sometimes for a while in the evenings but she was always home come meal time. She didn't take any of her meals out. And she was most always home and in for the evening by nine o'clock."

"You know if she met anybody, got to know people? Besides your guests, that is."

"Not to my knowledge and I wouldn't be expecting her to."

Fellows arched an eyebrow. "You wouldn't?"

"Well I should tell you about that. Like I say, she was reserved and quiet but that was in the beginning. She was a friendly girl and I think she needed friends. After she was with us four or five days she opened up quite a bit and after a while she got to talk to me quite a lot about herself." Mrs. Fremont's face became sad again. "She was a widow, poor thing. Her husband was killed in an automobile accident only three months ago and she was very lonely. She told me she'd been very much in love with her husband and you could see it when she talked about him. Her eyes'd get moist.

"She said she was trying to make some sense out of her life, trying to pull herself together. Henry, that's her husband, his loss had been such a shock. It was so unexpected. What she wanted to do, she said, was get away from family. That's his family. She didn't have no family of her own. She'd been living with them since her husband's death and she wanted to get away by herself for a little while."

"Mrs. Henry Moore," Fellows said. "Elizabeth Moore. Whereabouts is the husband's family?"

Mrs. Fremont hesitated. "Well I don't know exactly. Leastways she never happened to mention it but I'm pretty sure it's Pittsfield. Anyway, that's where the letter come from."

"She got a letter?"

Mrs. Fremont nodded firmly. "Yes, sir, but I'm sure that letter wasn't family."

"Why? She tell you about it?"

"No, sir. She didn't say a word about the letter but it was written by a man. It was a man's handwriting on the face of that envelope and it had an effect on her. I could tell that when I gave it to her. It kind of tensed her up, nervous like. It wasn't much but I could see she knew who it was from the minute she laid eyes on it and it was sort of as if she wasn't sure she was going to like what was inside."

"Let's talk about this letter a little," Fellows said. "Was there a return address on it?"

"No return address, but the postmark said Pittsfield, August twenty-ninth, the day before she got it."

"Do you remember the envelope?"

"I do. It was light gray. Man's writing paper. Good quality. I don't mean real expensive, but it wasn't cheap stationery."

Fellows noted that and looked up. "And you have no idea who sent it except you're pretty sure it wasn't family?"

Mrs. Fremont said archly, "Now I didn't say I don't have no idea who sent it. I only said she didn't *tell* me."

"Then what's your idea?"

Mrs. Fremont leaned forward a little. "Betty was telling me, after she opened up and got over being shy, that her husband had a close friend. He was best man at the wedding, in fact. Well, she said, this close friend of her late husband's was starting to get amorous. In fact, she hinted to me that he didn't wait till her husband was dead but that he'd been giving her some trouble even before her husband was killed. She said she was nervous about him and maybe she used the word 'nervous' but I could tell what she really meant was she was afraid of him." Mrs.

Fremont plumped her hands in her lap and sat up a little
straighter. "Now I'll tell you something else. She didn't say this,
mind you, but I got the very definite impression that this wanting to get away and be alone wasn't so much a matter of getting away from her husband's family as it was getting away from
her husband's best friend. Now that's what I mean about who
that letter was from and that's why I think her husband's family
lives in Pittsfield because if the letter is from the best friend
and he's in Pittsfield and he was giving her trouble when she was
with the family, then the family lives in Pittsfield. You see?"

"I see," Fellows said. "What I don't see is why she'd be giving
her address to a man she wanted to get away from. Presumably
this would have been after she moved into your place."

Mrs. Fremont couldn't help him on that. Betty, she told him,
had said absolutely nothing about that letter.

Fellows said, "Well, we'll look into it," and made more notes.
"Now how about Betty's behavior yesterday? Can you tell us
about that?"

"That I can," she answered with a knowing nod. "Like I told
you, that letter she got, it was mailed in Pittsfield on Thursday
and she got it Friday. So she says nothing about it and that's
important right there because she'd been telling me things and
here is the first and only piece of mail that come for her the
time she's been staying with me and she's mum. She's completely
mum.

"Now then, yesterday everything was the same as usual. That's
all day long, up through dinner and all. And then it comes
around half past eight or thereabouts and down the stairs comes
Betty and she's all decked out. She's got her prettiest dress on
and her heels and she's got her makeup on and her hair all
brushed and she's turned out just as pretty as a picture and she
says to me she might be late getting home because she has a date
at nine o'clock!"

Mrs. Fremont slapped her hand on the table. "Well, you
could've bowled me over. She hadn't gone out nights, she hadn't
done much of anything. So I'll tell you my first thought was
surprise because I didn't think she'd got to meet anybody and

then my second thought was that it was nice to see her look like that, be interested in having a date again. I must say I didn't give it a moment's thought at the time that her getting dolled up to go out had anything to do with that letter she got the day before. But as soon as I heard about the murder and got pretty dead sure it was Betty who was the one who got killed, why then I remembered that letter." She pointed a finger. "And I'll tell you, Mister Chief, I don't think for a second that date was with anybody else but the one who wrote it to her!"

Fellows noted the information and looked up. "When she went out was she wearing her wristwatch, the one with the diamonds?"

"Oh, yes. She wore that everywhere. It was a gift from her husband, she told me."

"And how did she appear when she was going out for her date, Mrs. Fremont? Did she seem excited, nervous, happy, or what?"

"Excited, I'd say," she answered after a pause. "Keyed up a little."

"Glad?"

"Well I don't know that I'd call her glad."

"You thought at first it was with some boy she'd met in—ah —Little Bohemia?"

Mrs. Fremont smiled. "You don't have to apologize for calling it Little Bohemia. We even do ourselves now. It's got no other name."

"All right, but you thought at the time she was glad to be having the date?"

"Well, I guess I did at the time. Maybe now that I think about it she might have been nervous instead of happy."

Fellows compressed his lips. "Did she at any time happen to mention the name of this best friend? She call him anything?"

Mrs. Fremont shook her head. "Nope. She never did, more's the pity."

"And her husband was killed in an automobile accident three months ago? She tell you any of the details?"

"Not how it happened, no. She just said he was killed in a car accident. Didn't say if there was another car or what."

"When she went out of the house every day, what did she do?"

"Don't know. Walked around, I guess. She didn't buy things that I know of, except magazines. Leastways I never saw her bring home any packages. If you want my opinion she didn't want to stay cooped up in her room all the time."

Fellows glanced up. "Sid?"

Wilks had no additional questions. "We'd like to see her room though."

"Oh, yes," Mrs. Fremont said, rising. "Be my guest."

CHAPTER VII

Mrs. Fremont's boarding and tourist home was on Number Three Street, as the short cross-streets were named. It was a large rambling frame house with weathered shingles, white trim, a red door and blue door frame.

The late Betty Moore's room was at the rear down a long second floor hall that opened onto half a dozen bedrooms. Mrs. Fremont led the way over creaking boards in an otherwise silent house. Most of the eighteen guests were out but one or two of the more permanent residents peeked from their rooms furtively at the arrival of the police.

Betty's room was locked but Mrs. Fremont had the key and threw the door open to reveal its small interior. There was an iron bed, a dresser, closet, small table and an easy chair with a flowered cover. A large throw rug covered the brown painted boards of the floor and two south windows looked into the house next door.

Fellows and Wilks studied the room from the doorway and

Mrs. Fremont said, "This is just how she left it. I didn't touch a thing. I just looked in."

Fellows thanked her and asked if she'd prepare a list of guests who'd known Mrs. Moore. "We'd also appreciate it if you'd let us have the page in the register that bears her signature."

"I'll get right about it," she said, starting off, and the two policemen closed the door after her. Wilks went to the old iron double bed, pulled down the covers carefully, lifted the mattress for a look and got down on his knees to peer at the dusty floor underneath.

Fellows picked up three movie magazines and two paperback books which were doctor-nurse hospital romances. The books were worn and a pencilled notation on the flyleaf of each said, "10¢". "Secondhand," he said as Wilks came over. "Probably bought them here at one of the bookstores. The magazines are new. I imagine she got those here too."

Wilks flipped through the magazines rapidly, looking for writing, and laid them in place again. "Romantic literature. Trying to escape the dreariness of her own life, I guess."

Fellows glanced around at the drab furnishings, the glass-shaded overhead light, the water stains on the ceiling. "I guess she was trying to escape a lot of things. Only she didn't quite make it."

"The case of the amorous best man? I'm beginning to wonder if the husband's death was as much an accident as the girl thought."

"That idea occurred to me too," Fellows said. "It wouldn't hurt to check with Motor Vehicles." He turned to the bureau drawers and pulled them out one after the other. The two bottom ones were empty and all the girl's belongings were in the top. There were some underthings, a box of new stockings, two pairs of ankle socks, box of tissues, four handkerchiefs, two blouses, brush and comb and a plastic kit of toilet articles.

The chief lifted and poked the items, picked up the blouses and studied them. "No laundry marks," he said, putting them back. He upended the toilet kit on the bureau top and sorted the contents. They consisted of toothbrush and paste, a vial of

perfume, deodorant, aspirin, half a bottle of dramamine, sham-
poo, three packets of bath salts, Q-Tips and Band-aids. "Looks
like the girl went on a ship someplace or took a plane trip," he
said, holding up the dramamine. "What's in the closet?"

Wilks, looking through things there, said, "Nothing much.
The blue linen suit she wore, two skirts, pair of sandals and a
suitcase. No labels on the clothes. They look as if she might
have made them herself."

"Domestic type, maybe? Any initials on the suitcase?"

Wilks brought it out. "No initials but it was a sea trip she
took. There's the remains of a sticker."

"Legible?" Fellows asked, going over.

"No. She scrubbed most of it off." Wilks opened the suitcase
on the bed, looked through pockets and felt the lining. "Wood,"
he said. "Cloth cover. Leather trim. No secret compartments.
Brass fittings. Small, overnight-type bag, moderately expensive.
Just about carry what she's got here and it's not very much."

"She traveled light," Fellows agreed. "She had nothing in the
pockets of her suit?"

"Nothing. Nothing tucked in her shoes, nothing on the
closet shelf."

Fellows nodded thoughtfully. He turned and picked up the
wastebasket for a closer examination but all that was in it was a
Kleenex with lipstick on it, hairs from her brush and an empty
bath salt packet. He glanced around again, then went to the
lone decoration in the room, a framed reproduction of a fishing
wharf in watercolor. He took it off the hook, looked at the back,
found nothing and hung it again. He looked behind the dresser
mirror with the same results.

Wilks, watching, said, "Are you hunting for something in particular?"

"I hoped she might have that letter around," Fellows answered, "or an address or something written on a slip of paper.
I guess she carried that letter in her purse. And it looks as though
she carried all her money in her purse too. I wonder how much
of it she had."

Wilks smiled. "You still working on that robbery motive?"

Fellows shrugged. "I'm not considering motives until I talk to that amorous best man." He looked around one last time with his hands on his hips. "Well, there's nothing more here. We might as well pack her things and see what the lab can do with them and you can start questioning some of these guests."

It was quarter past two when the chief got back to headquarters with the dead girl's suitcase. No reports on the case were waiting for him but four reporters were. "About time you got in, Chief," they said. "You been keeping us waiting. That's no way to get your name spelled right."

"I forgot about you boys," Fellows told them. "I thought since most of you wouldn't be publishing tomorrow you'd be lying on a beach somewhere."

"Speaking of lying on the beach—"

Fellows answered questions about the case then, frankly and as fully as required. He told them the dead girl was Mrs. Elizabeth Moore, a recent widow, presumably from Pittsfield. She'd lived in Mrs. Fremont's boarding house since August twenty-third, had received a letter on Friday and had gone out on a date Saturday night. The man she had had the date with was the man they were looking for. They also wanted to speak to the girl's in-laws and with her late husband's best friend. They'd have pictures of the girl for release shortly, probably tomorrow.

"What's in the suitcase, Chief?"

"The girl's belongings."

"Can we see them?"

"If it's important you can, but you aren't allowed to touch."

"Sure it's important. That's the kind of thing that lends color to a story. Young murder victim moves into her new home with nothing but the clothes on her back. All she owns in the world fits into one small suitcase. Then we tell just exactly what it was she did own, what kind of toothpaste she used."

Fellows smiled and since there was nothing that required his immediate attention, he obliged the press and let them itemize the possessions the girl had left behind. He saw them out the door fifteen minutes later and repacked the bag. "I sometimes think I'm a damned fool," he said to Sergeant Unger.

"Like a fox," Unger told him. "There's not a cop in the country who's got a better press than you have."

"I'm not interested in what kind of a press I've got. What's important is if I cooperate with them they cooperate with me and that's damned necessary sometimes. Here. Call in one of the cars, will you, and have them take this bag to the State Police barracks. It's to go to the lab."

Fellows went into his office then and put in a belated call to Chief Crouch of the Pittsfield police. Crouch was another who had known Fellows' cooperation and was glad to reciprocate. Fellows outlined the case to him and said, "We'd like the help of your department in tracing a family named Moore in your town who lost a son in an automobile accident three months ago."

"Sure," Crouch said genially. "That won't be hard. Put a couple of men on it right away. Anything else?"

"Yes. We want the name of the best man at the son's wedding. Right now he looks like a suspect. Also, we'd like all information the Moores can give you on the accident itself, the one in which the son was killed. Specifically I'm curious about the possibility of its not being an accident."

"You think somebody had a grudge against both the husband and wife, huh? You think it might be a double murder?"

"Something like that."

Crouch promised an answer by morning and Fellows, with the murder taken care of for the moment, turned to routine matters, the complaints, the problems, the ordinary affairs that involved the small Stockford force.

The interlude was brief. At quarter past three Patrolman William Hogarth, who'd been called in to trace the bus driver, reported. The driver, he said, remembered and described Betty Moore and said he picked her up at Center and Meadow on his three o'clock run. She asked for Little Bohemia and he let her off there ten minutes later. He knew nothing more about her.

Fellows added that piece of information to the sparse file on Betty's background and gave Hogarth his next assignment. It was to question the driver of the intercity bus from Pittsfield that would have dropped the girl in Stockford and see what he could add. "There's less chance he'll remember her, but her picture might do it. See what you can get."

A final call came in for the chief a half-hour later. It was from Dr. MacFarlane, the medical examiner. "I haven't completed the autopsy," the doctor said, "and I can't tell you the time of death yet, but I thought you'd like to know. The girl had sexual relations before she was killed."

Fellows, with one of the proofs of the dead girl on the desk before him, nodded without surprise. "I expected she had," he said. "Only one thing. Are you sure it's *before?*"

"You mean, might he have strangled her first and then committed the act? That's possible. Maybe I'd be more correct in saying she had relations around the time of death."

"That would make it on the beach where she was found, then?"

"Presumably."

"Um-hmm," Fellows said thoughtfully. "And you don't know the cause of death for sure?"

"It's almost certainly strangulation but I'll give you a definite answer tomorrow."

"O.K., Jim. Sorry to spoil your weekend."

"That's as nothing compared to what got spoiled for that girl. She's a young, pretty thing. It's too bad."

"I know," Fellows said and a corner of his mouth tightened. "It's always too bad. If she'd played it different; if she hadn't gone out with him; if she hadn't let him take her to the beach; if a lot of things." He sighed. "No matter how long I stay in this business I never get used to the idea of people killing people."

CHAPTER VIII

Labor Day dawned with a baleful sun and promised to be as hot as the day before. At Indian Lake the crowds came early and by half past ten the beach and pavilion were overrun. Six hundred cars glistened in the parking lot and only in the farthest reaches were there spaces for more. In Little Bohemia, slacks, shorts and bathing suits were the order of the day and the streets teemed with natives, tourists, visitors and renters, all wandering among the shops and artists' studios in their bright-colored sports shirts and half-buttoned blouses.

In with the early members of the horde descending on the small resort area were patrolmen Cassidy, Raphael and Dzanowski and Detective Sergeant Sid Wilks. They were back to continue the investigation into Betty Moore, only this time they came armed with her picture. Part of the assignment was to show the picture at every public concession and shop for Betty was pretty enough to make an impression and Fellows was certain that where she'd been she'd be remembered. With luck they might turn up someone who would also remember the man who had been with her Saturday night and produce a description.

While the hunt for the man's description was going on, Fellows sat in his office waiting to learn his identity. To the chief it was a routine case. The Pittsfield police would locate the dead girl's in-laws and from them get the name of the amorous best man. He'd be picked up for questioning and, with proper handling, would confess. That was the way with most murder cases. You find a body. You talk to people. You learn who wanted the victim dead. You bring him in and he tells the story.

At nine o'clock that morning, however, the Betty Moore murder case dropped from the ranks of the routine. Chief Crouch got on the wire to Fellows and said, by way of opening, "You got the wrong city, Fellows. We been through the whole of Pittsfield and there ain't any family named Moore who's lost a son in a smashup three months ago. In fact, none of the Moores in town have lost any sons, Henry or otherwise, in a smashup any time!" ·

"Damn it," Fellows said, jerking his chair upright. "You're sure of that?"

"There ain't a Moore in town we didn't get to."

Fellows rubbed his chin and made a face. "Do any of them have sons named Henry?" he asked, groping.

"One does but he's not married to any girl called Betty. He's only eleven years old."

"That's not so good. That kind of complicates things."

Crouch tried to be sympathetic. "Well listen, Fellows. From what you told me yesterday you're only assuming the girl's in-laws live here. It's only because the letter was postmarked here, ain't that right?"

"Yes, that's right. We've been guessing the letter was from this amorous best man she was afraid of but of course it might not have been. But it was postmarked 'Pittsfield' so somebody in your town must have known where she was."

"That may be, Fellows, but what's that tell you? There's a hundred and seventy thousand people in this city."

"And that letter," Fellows went on musingly, "was the only piece of mail she received in ten days. It doesn't sound as if she let too many people know where she was going to be. If it's not the amorous friend, who was the man she knew well enough to give her address to?"

"Or," Crouch reminded him, "was smart enough to find it out. Don't sound likely to me she'd give her address to some guy who wanted to kill her."

Crouch wasn't the brightest chief of police in the country but there was a certain basic logic to his thinking. Fellows smiled and said, "Yes, there's that angle, of course. Anyway, I guess this

may take a little longer than I thought. It looks as though we'll
have to go to the Pittsfield marriage records."

"We can do that for you," Crouch offered. "Tell me what
you want."

"That would help. Thanks. What I want is a girl named
Elizabeth marrying somebody named Moore. They may have
moved out of town while the amorous friend still lives there."

"We'll take care of it. Of course we can't today."

"I know. These damned holidays. I want to check with Motor
Vehicles about Henry's accident and that has to wait till tomorrow too. And, of course, a lot of papers don't publish today
which makes it tough circulating the girl's picture."

"Damned holidays is right," Crouch said. "We've had three
accident calls already."

Hogarth was the next to phone in and he had more bad news.
He had talked and shown Betty's picture to all bus drivers who
could have picked the girl up in Pittsfield and dropped her in
Stockford before three o'clock August twenty-third and none
could remember her. "They think I'm crazy," he said, "asking
about passengers they carried a week ago. They don't even know
who got on and off their last run."

Fellows wasn't surprised. "It was just a chance," he said. "I
hoped she might have asked them a question the way she did
the local driver and get herself remembered that way."

"Well, I guess she knew how to get to Stockford all right because I tried that angle. Whichever bus she came on she didn't
do anything to call attention to herself."

Nothing more developed until noon when Sid Wilks called
in. He reported that he'd now covered all of Mrs. Fremont's
guests and they could shed but little further light on the dead
girl. "One of them recalled her saying she and her husband traveled around a lot, that's all."

"It's not much," Fellows told him. "What are you doing,
chewing?"

"Yeah. A salami sandwich. I'm at the pavilion. They make
good ones."

"How can you eat stuff like that and not put on weight?"

"I exercise. After talking to those guests I hiked about thirty miles showing Betty's picture all over the beach. It's great for the waistline."

"Never mind your waistline, what'd you find out?"

"Nothing. But nothing. There's a million fish here and not one bite. Some of the people were at the pavilion Saturday night and others have been in other days but it's no dice. Nobody recognizes her. If she had a plain face I wouldn't expect much but with a face like hers—well, the men would remember her, damn it."

"Maybe that means they really didn't see her."

"Why the hell wouldn't they see her? She wasn't invisible."

Fellows tilted back in his chair. "They couldn't see her if she didn't ever go to the pavilion."

"Where else would a guy take a date in this place?"

"Out on the beach so he could kill her."

"Her date was for nine o'clock. She probably wasn't killed till close to midnight. How did they spend their time?"

"Remember the cord around her neck, Sid? The boy didn't pick it up off the beach. He had it on him. If he had plans to use that cord he's not going to want to be seen with her beforehand."

"I see," Wilks said drily. "He's planning to murder her and then throws in a rape job as an afterthought?"

"Maybe. And maybe he throws in a robbery job as an after-afterthought."

"That's some beaut of a date she had. I wonder how a girl like her could get to know a man like that."

"So do I, and it doesn't look as though we'll find out in a hurry." He went on to explain about the bus drivers and Crouch's failure to find Betty's in-laws in Pittsfield.

Wilks wasn't upset by the news. "Don't worry about it," he said. "The Moores might not live in Pittsfield but they're not going to be very far away. Betty Moore came down to Little Bohemia, don't forget. That means she knew what it was and where it was and nobody who doesn't live in or near Stockford would ever have heard of it. Which reminds me. Have you checked the Moores in Stockford?"

"There're only two of them. Jim and his cousin."

"Just checking up on you. Well, I'm going to hang around a while longer and catch the late-comers when they park. Hey, I just thought of something. In-town cars with stickers park free but all out-of-town cars have to pay a buck. It's a long shot but the parking attendant might just possibly remember collecting a buck from the kind of guy Betty might have a date with at about nine o'clock Saturday night."

"It's worth a try," Fellows agreed. "That guy didn't materialize out of thin air. He left tracks and that might be one of them."

CHAPTER IX

Betty Moore, in her lonely stay at Mrs. Fremont's, filled her time not only with the reading of romantic magazines but with the movies. Joseph Dzanowski relayed that information to the chief shortly after one o'clock Labor Day afternoon. The ticket taker at Little Bohemia's tiny theater identified Betty as a girl who had spent nearly every afternoon at the show even though it meant seeing the same picture three days running.

"Was she alone or in company?" Fellows asked him.

"Always alone," Dzanowski replied. "Always alone, the poor little girl, except the one time she should have stayed alone."

This revelation helped account for the girl's activities during her stay at Mrs. Fremont's but it shed no light on the fatal night. Fellows' conviction, however, remained strong that the mysterious stranger Betty had gone to meet could not have passed through and around Little Bohemia totally unobserved and persistent questioning would eventually turn up somebody who would remember him.

In this he was right but it wasn't from Wilks or the other policemen that the first breaks came. At ten minutes of two that afternoon a young man, John Carlson of 66 King Street, and a girl, Linda Waters of 46 Douglas Street, presented themselves at police headquarters, hand-in-hand, to report that they had heard about the murder and thought they had seen the man.

Carlson, a thin, sandy-haired youth, did the talking. He and Linda went dancing at the pavilion Saturday night, he told the chief. At about half past nine they decided to go down on the beach and look at the moon. They wandered way up near the far end, past everybody else so far as they knew, and there they relaxed on the sand, watched the moon and talked until quarter past eleven.

"It was along about ten-thirty—." He turned to the girl. "Right, Hon?"

Linda, who had reddish hair, freckles, glasses, and slightly protruding teeth, said, "Well I wasn't watching the time but I'd guess that was about right. Maybe twenty of eleven. Do you think?"

Carlson nodded. "Ten thirty, twenty of eleven, around in there. Anyway, along the beach comes this couple, a girl and a boy. They had their arms around each other. We couldn't see them too well, of course, and I don't know what the girl looked like—"

Fellows said, "Hold on a moment," and went back to his office to get Betty's picture. The couple studied it and the boy said, "It could be the girl, right, Hon?"

Hon nodded. "Could be." She turned. "Like Johnny says, we couldn't see them too well."

"Was the moon under a cloud?" Fellows asked.

"No, not right then," the lad put in. "But we were back on the beach and they were going along the middle. Like I say, they had their arms around each other and their faces were kind of in shadow. Anyway, they went by towards the end of the beach and we didn't think any more about it, at least for a while, right, Hon?"

"I forgot about them to tell the God's truth," the girl said.

"That's right. We forgot about them until—what would you say, Hon, eleven o'clock?"

"That would be about right. I wasn't paying any real attention to the time, of course."

"About eleven. Then we hear this girl up the beach where they'd went. She suddenly says, 'No. No.'"

The youth stopped and waited. Fellows said, " 'No. No.', eh? Is that all? Just 'No. No.'?"

"That's all. After that there was dead silence."

"Did it sound as if she was in trouble?"

The boy flushed a little. "Well, it was—I thought—she just said those two words and she didn't say anything else and I thought—"

"You didn't go see if she needed help?"

Carlson wet his lips. "I didn't think—I didn't want to butt in." He flushed still more. "You see, what I thought was—uh—that maybe he was trying to do something the girl didn't want him to. But then when she didn't say anything more I just sort of assumed he'd stopped."

"Or," put in Linda, "that she'd changed her mind."

Fellows said, "What happened after that?"

"Nothing. Everything was quiet after that."

"How long did you stay?"

"Like I said, till about quarter past. I remember it was twenty-five past when we got back to the pavilion."

"The boy didn't come back in the meantime?"

"No. They were still up at the end of the beach so far as we know."

"He couldn't have gone by without your seeing him?"

Both John and Linda shook their heads. "We would have seen him."

Fellows was silent for a few moments making notes. The boy said, "Do you think he was the murderer?"

The chief looked up. "It sounds likely. Can you tell me exactly where you were and exactly where this other couple was?"

"We were about seventy-five to a hundred yards from the far end of the beach, right, Hon?"

"Closer to a hundred," the girl answered.

"Yes, about a hundred and they went well past us. The girl didn't sound too near when she said, 'No. No.' "

"How far away would you guess she was?"

"Maybe forty yards."

"Closer to fifty," Hon said.

"That's close enough," Fellows said. "So between ten thirty and ten forty a couple passed you going near the end of the beach and twenty minutes to half an hour later the girl cries out, 'No. No.' After that there's silence for another fifteen minutes, at which point you leave?"

"That's about right, right, Hon?"

Fellows said, "Can you describe the man?"

Carlson scratched his head dubiously. "Not too well. We couldn't see his face."

"Was he tall, short, thin, fat, dark, light?"

"Tall and slender, right, Hon? And dark."

Fellows looked at the girl and she nodded. "They looked like lovers. We never dreamed he was going to kill her! If we had, John would have stopped him."

John nodded. "I thought it was something else. I mean we felt a little uncomfortable. That's why we left."

CHAPTER X

A second couple who had been on the beach that night appeared at headquarters later in the afternoon with another tale to relate. The girl, an attractive blonde with a large engagement ring, was the obvious instigator and her fiance, a good-looking, dark-haired youth named Hank Wilson, was more in tow than with her. "We've got something to tell you," the girl said. "It's about Saturday night. The night of the murder."

She gave her name as Adele Edmunds and Fellows took down an address on exclusive Bungalow Road while the youth shifted his feet uncomfortably and said, "It's really nothing."

"It is *too* something," Adele told him. "The police want everybody to help whether they've got anything or not. Isn't that right?"

Fellows allowed as how it was and took the youth's address. That, it turned out, was the Savannah House on Number Four Street in Little Bohemia and Fellows, as a matter of course, produced the inevitable picture of Betty in a try for recognition. That gave Adele a chance to say, "You see? Didn't I tell you? We don't know what's important!"

The boy, however, shook his head and said he hadn't seen her around. "Of course I'm not around much myself. I'm at Adele's house most of the time anyway." He gave her a superior look and said, "So there. I told you so."

"That's got nothing to do with this," she retorted and turned to Fellows. "We," she said dramatically, "were down on the beach the night of the murder!"

"It was way *after* the murder," Wilson put in. "It doesn't mean a thing."

"That depends," Fellows said, "on when the murder was committed."

"Well the television says it was between ten and twelve," Adele answered. "That's right, isn't it?"

"And we didn't go out on the beach till after that," Wilson told her.

"We went out on the beach just before twelve. You know that very well. And the murder might not have been committed till twelve o'clock. You keep saying it must have happened before we went out there and I keep telling you it might not have."

"What's the difference?" the boy complained. "We weren't anywhere *near* where it happened."

"Nevertheless, we should go to the police even if all we were was around. Isn't that right, sir?"

Fellows said, "Yes, that's right. Now let's get it straight. Would you tell me what you did in detail?"

"We were dancing in the pavilion," the youth said. "We danced until twelve o'clock and then went down to the beach."

"Before twelve," Adele insisted.

"Whereabouts did you go?" Fellows wanted to know.

"Only about a hundred yards up," Wilson said.

"A hundred and fifty," Adele amended.

Fellows sighed. "I wish you two would get your stories straight."

"Let me tell it," Adele said. "You didn't want to come anyway. We went out on the beach a little before twelve and we were there for about an hour. Until they closed up the pavilion."

Fellows nodded. "You see anybody while you were out there?"

"A couple of couples went by."

"Which way?"

"I don't exactly remember. Coming in, I think, towards the pavilion."

"There might have been more," the youth said. "It was cloudy most of the time."

Fellows waited but neither volunteered anything else. "Is that all there is to the story?" he asked.

Adele looked a little let down. "I guess so."

"I told you we shouldn't bother the police," Wilson said.

"She did right," Fellows told him. "Every bit helps. The main thing is you only saw couples. Is that right? You didn't see any single men?"

The boy said no but the girl suddenly snapped her fingers. "We did too. Remember? The one who shined the flashlight on us. You swore at him."

"Yeah," the slim youth conceded and smiled for a change. "Some crackpot."

Fellows' manner didn't change but the sharpness of his eye was honed a little. "Tell me about this crackpot," he said.

Adele did the telling. "It was around half past twelve and we

were on the beach—well you might as well know—smooching."
She waved the large diamond. "We're engaged as you can see."

Wilson made a face at the term "smooching" but the girl
was nothing if not forthright. "When all of a sudden this flashlight shined on us. I jumped a foot. I thought it was a cop—I
mean I thought—well, anyway, it turned out to be some boy.
Hank sat up and swore and the boy quickly turned off the light
and went on."

"What direction was he headed?"

"Up the beach. Towards the far end."

"Away from the pavilion, towards the site of the murder?"

"That's right. The moon was out but it was behind him so we
couldn't see his face, especially with the flashlight in our eyes,
but he had a lightweight jacket on and he was, well, not as tall
as Hank but rather tall and kind of stocky."

"Any idea of his age?"

"I got the impression he was young. Maybe twenty. Maybe
even younger."

"Did you see him shine the light anywhere else?"

Adele shook her head. "No," she confessed frankly. "We resumed smooching and forgot about him. In fact, I didn't remember until you asked." She looked hopefully at the chief. "Do
you think that's important?"

"I think it might be."

He saw the couple out and came back to Sergeant Unger.
"Pass the word when the patrols report in. I want inquiries made
at the pavilion and around Little Bohemia for a stocky youth
seen Saturday night with a flashlight. I also want one of our men
down on that beach tonight in case he shows up again."

Unger smiled. "Won't that chase everybody away?"

"I'll have him take his wife along."

Unger laughed. "I guess that would be a real thrill, Chief." He
added, more soberly, "You think this kid with the flashlight is a
suspect?"

"That's what I want to find out. Was he the murderer come
back to find something he dropped? Was he a kid wandering far

enough up the beach with his flashlight to stumble on the body? Find him and we'll find some answers."

Two more reports came in that afternoon. Wilks phoned to say the parking attendant remembered nothing and that he'd shown Betty's picture to more countless numbers of people without results. Fellows told him about the stocky lad and Wilks said he'd make inquiries.

The final report was phoned in by Dr. MacFarlane, the written report to follow. Elizabeth Moore, he said, had died of strangulation. Time of death was between eleven and eleven thirty Saturday evening with ten forty-five and eleven forty-five the outside limits. "You heard from Avery about an inquest yet?"

"Not a word. I'm told he's away for the holiday."

"What do you want me to do with the girl's personal effects?"

"They go to the State Police lab. What does she have specifically?"

"One dress, one slip, one bra, two shoes and half a dozen bobby pins."

"What about the cord she was strangled with?"

"If you want to call that a personal effect. I'm sending that to the lab in any event. I removed it without touching the knot."

"Thanks, Jim. And thanks for all the rest."

"It's my job," MacFarlane said simply. "You don't have to thank me."

"I will all the same. You get her teeth?"

"Teeth and fingerprints. That's part of the job. The prints are on their way to Hartford already."

CHAPTER XI

The newspapers which didn't publish on Labor Day got their first shot at the three-day old murder on Tuesday, September third and they made up for lost time. Betty Moore's picture ran two columns wide on the front pages with the cutlines describing her as the "widowed beauty" found strangled on the beach. The stories dealt with her background as revealed by Mrs. Fremont, the accent being on the mysterious letter and the amorous best man. How long she had been married and where she had lived was still a matter of conjecture but the facts regarding the discovery of her death were elaborately described.

Two angles which all the papers played up that day made Fellows unhappy. One was the story of the youth with the flashlight which an enterprising reporter had got from Adele Edmunds. This, Fellows had withheld from the press to avoid chasing the youth into hiding but it was there on the front pages anyway. The other was the best man bit. The chief would have liked to seek the amorous friend without letting him know he was a major suspect but Mrs. Fremont was beyond control and she had been fulsome in her dealings with the press, holding back nothing, including her suspicions.

"Damn prying reporters anyway," Fellows growled. "How the hell did they learn the Edmunds girl was in here?"

The hunt for the stocky youth with the flashlight was being pressed and Wilks went down to the pavilion again that morning. The season was over and the place closing for the winter but Morrie Leibman was there with three other employees cleaning up and Morrie had some information. It wasn't Saturday, he said, but a kid with a flashlight was in the soda room Friday night. Morrie, in fact, had served him and asked what the light was for. The boy had said he was going to look for night-crawlers.

Leibman described him as a heavyset youth, brown hair and eyes, brown slacks, plaid sportshirt and a light zipper jacket. The flashlight protruded from the pocket of the jacket. "Five ten, a hundred and eighty," was Leibman's best estimate of the boy's size and he guessed his age at nineteen.

Wilks reported this to Fellows in his office around eleven and said, "This guy Leibman says he's seen the kid before during the summer. He can't say he always carries a flashlight."

"He lives in the area then?"

"I don't know. Leibman lives in Little Bohemia himself but he doesn't remember seeing him there. I talked to the lifeguards but they don't know anything about it. If you want anything else from those lifeguards, by the way, you'd better tell me fast. They were in their rooms packing when I found them and they're getting the first train out."

"We've got their home addresses," Fellows said. "So, if Leibman is reliable, this kid with the flashlight probably doesn't live in Little Bohemia but he probably does live in Stockford."

"That's my guess." Wilks poured some coffee from the chief's thermos into a cup, looked and said, "Oh damn. It's another diet day. No milk and sugar."

"You want me to tell you what I weighed this morning?"

"I'd rather hear what you think of the kid. He doesn't fit the description of the man seen walking arm-in-arm with the dead girl twenty minutes before she was killed."

"Now what kind of a description did we get of that man, for the love of Pete? Tall, dark, slender. I could've walked down onto that beach yesterday afternoon and picked up fifty tall, dark, slender young men in five minutes."

"Sure you could, but you wouldn't have picked up a stocky youth with brown hair carrying a flashlight."

"That doesn't let the kid off the hook. How good a description are you going to get from a couple of neckers on the beach? Who's to say brown hair isn't black hair in the moonlight at thirty feet? Who's to say whether a man is slender or stocky when he and a girl are walking with their arms around each other's waists? And if he's not the guy the couple described he still might be connected. Maybe he goes around picking up single girls. Maybe Betty's date never showed up. Maybe he left her for a minute and the kid came along. After all, we can't be positive the couple young Mr. 'Right, Hon' and his Hon saw was Betty Moore and her date. We can't be sure the letter she got has any place in the picture. We can't be sure it was from the amorous best man. Hell, we can't even be sure there ever was a Betty Moore."

"Except," Wilks said drily, "for a certain dissected corpse down in the basement of the hospital."

"That's right," Fellows said, pouring some coffee into his own cup. "But why haven't we heard from her in-laws? She's in all the papers now and it's eleven o'clock. Somebody who knows her ought to be calling in."

"They might have been away for the weekend. Give them more time."

Fellows made a face. "If they take much more time I'll hear about them from Motor Vehicles before I hear from them themselves. And if I do, they'd better have a good excuse ready."

The Moores were not heard from that afternoon but a number of other people were. A young man named Bill Jacobs came in during his lunch hour to report that he was down on the beach with a girl Friday night and somebody had flashed a light on him for two or three seconds. It was overcast and he didn't get a look at who it was but the assumption could be made that it was the same stocky youth Morrie Leibman had seen.

County Coroner Clement Avery called up in the early afternoon but stalled on setting a date for the inquest. "I need more of a direction to point a finger," he complained to the chief, "than some nebulous best man at a wedding you can't find out anything about or some mysterious boy with a flashlight."

A short time later there was a report from the Pittsfield police that caused Fellows' eyes to widen a little. A check of the marriage records revealed four men named Moore marrying girls named Elizabeth but none of the four had anything to do with the girl on the beach. Wherever Betty Moore had married her husband, it wasn't in Pittsfield.

Even more startling, however, was the call from the Motor Vehicle Department. In the whole of Connecticut in the whole of the year no man named Henry Moore had died in a vehicular accident.

This bit of news left Fellows completely nonplussed and he was still frowning over it when Wilks returned from a fruitless round of questions down at the beach.

"I don't get it," Fellows said when he had finished filling in the detective sergeant on the various reports. "I don't understand any of this at all."

"It's not hard," Wilks told him, sitting back and biting off some chewing tobacco. "The couple did not get married in Pittsfield as you thought. The husband was not killed in Connecticut as you thought. The answer is they got married and he got killed in some other state as you have not thought."

"Sure, I know that much. But what about the in-laws?"

"They don't live in this state either."

"So where did the girl get married and where do the in-laws live? In some town that has no radio, television or newspapers?"

Wilks sat up and gestured idly. "Maybe she got married in Europe. Maybe her husband was a foreigner and she came back home after he died. Maybe she's a foreigner. There're a lot of reasons why we might not be hearing from the husband's family. Maybe the family doesn't like publicity. Maybe they threw her out of the house. Maybe they opposed her marriage to their son and sent her packing as soon as he was killed. Maybe they're glad she's dead. Maybe one of the family killed her. You want me to go on?"

Fellows shook his head and smiled. "That'll do for now. I guess the trouble with me is the heat and the disappointment. I thought this would be a cut and dried case and we'd wrap it up in a hurry." He sat up. "Apparently it's not as simple as it seems. Finding out who this girl is may be a real problem."

"Yeah, that's a complication all right. So, instead of finding out who killed her we have to find out who she is. Any report from Hartford on that? They got her prints on file?"

"I haven't heard yet but we should by tomorrow. If she's got a record, of course, we're all set."

"That's right," Wilks said, "but I have a sneaking suspicion the girl wasn't a criminal. I think that hope's going to fall flat."

Fellows slapped his hand on his desk. "Well, I'll tell you. Avery said since nobody's come forward to claim the body we can go ahead and bury it. Unless something happens between now and then, she's going to be buried tomorrow afternoon. Right now I think that's the way it's going to be. We're going to have a box out in the cemetery with an unidentified girl in it. There's going to be the name 'Elizabeth Moore' on the marker but that doesn't mean a damned thing. You might as well give her a number. So what this means is we're going to have a tough problem."

"That's already been decided on," Wilks said. "What are you sidling up to?"

"We're going to pursue every angle and I don't mean routine business like sending Harris and his wife down on the beach with the neckers every night and I don't mean contacting the motor vehicle departments of all the states from the Atlantic to the Pacific to find out where that accident was but I also mean the tough stuff."

"Such as?"

"I like what you said about Europe."

"You mean that she came from there?"

"Not that. I'm talking about that bottle of seasick pills we found in her belongings and the piece of sticker on her suitcase. She took a boat somewhere."

"And if it was to a foreign country, she'd have a passport?"

"That's part of it. We'll go after the passports all right, but there are plenty of places you can get to on a boat without needing a passport and that's what we're really going to concentrate on."

"You mean passenger lists?"

"That's right. I'm going to put Lewis, Daniels and Lerner on it, but I want you and Ed to set it up. Tomorrow the two of you are going down to New York and get the help of the New York police—if they can spare any help—and you'll contact the shipping lines and make the arrangements to see their lists and get the operation started. When that's done the others will start combing those lists for Elizabeth Moores."

CHAPTER XII

Wednesday morning saw Detective Sergeant Sidney Wilks and Plainclothesman Edward N. Lewis off for New York to set up the mammoth task of checking ship passenger lists. At the same time, other men were busy following other lines. Despite the fact that Henry Moore had not been killed in Connecticut, Fellows still held the view that Betty, in order to know there was a Little Bohemia, couldn't have come from too far away. The Moores, he felt, were somewhere near by and had failed to come forth for reasons other than ignorance of her fate. The family might not live in Pittsfield but he was sure they lived in a neighboring town and he spent a good part of the morning contacting local authorities in all surrounding communities for help in the hunt.

The boy with the flashlight, whom the papers had already nicknamed "The Flashlight Kid", had not appeared on the beach Tuesday night but Fellows was pushing the search for him hard too. Four of his own men were doing a canvass of Little Bohemia asking questions about such a youth.

The chief had a session with the newsmen at eleven o'clock but he had only one negative fact to give them. Hartford did not have the girl's fingerprints in its criminal records. "We didn't expect they would," he said, "so I don't know that we could call it a disappointment."

He gave them a rundown on the lines of investigation that were being followed, the stolen watch, the shipping lists, the motor vehicle departments, the hunt for the Moores, then answered questions.

"Do you think the Moores know the girl is dead?"

"With all the publicity you people have been giving her, I don't know why they wouldn't."

"Does that mean you think they haven't come forward because they don't want to be associated with her?"

Fellows smiled. "You're pushing. Ask the Moores when we find them."

At two o'clock that afternoon, the body which was the cause of so much activity but which, through it all, remained unclaimed and unmourned, was laid to rest in a spot reserved for the unknowns in the Heavenly Rest Cemetery on Nylandotte Road. Fellows attended the funeral and so did his wife, Cessie, but they were the only ones present other than the cemetery personnel involved and a volunteer minister from one of the churches in town.

When the brief service was over, the chief produced a small bouquet of flowers and placed it on the box, then took Cessie by the elbow and led her away. "I suppose that looks kind of silly," he said. "But you know, that's a sad way to go, all alone like that with nobody caring." He shook himself to shrug off the mood. "Anyway, thank God there weren't any reporters around."

Bad news was waiting for the chief when he got back to headquarters but there was a big piece of good news too. Five towns had failed to locate the missing in-laws but the "Flashlight Kid" had been found.

"Lambert turned him up," Unger told the chief. "Some woman thought he was the guy who palled around with a couple of her tenants and Lambert got the tenants to admit it. Kid by the name of Gordon Smith."

"Where is he?"

"John's gone to get him. The kid lives at twenty-nine Forest Street."

"Way up there, huh?"

"Quite a ways from Little Bohemia but Lambert says he's down there a lot palling around with these two other guys."

"Well," Fellows said, "there's a break for once and I can sure use one."

Gordon Smith made his appearance at headquarters three quarters of an hour later in the company of Patrolman Lambert. He was a huskily built youth in slacks and sportshirt and if he didn't enjoy being brought to police headquarters for questioning he didn't particularly resent it. He seemed, rather, to be interested in how the police went about such matters.

"Gordon Smith, eh?" Fellows said, coming out to look the boy over. "All right, let's go into the office and have a talk."

Smith offered no objections and followed obediently, taking the chair Fellows indicated. "Take notes, Lambert," the chief told the patrolman. He sat down at his desk, swinging his chair around to face the boy. "You talk to Mr. Lambert on your way down here, Smith?"

"Yes." The boy hooked an arm over the back of the chair, making himself comfortable.

"How old are you?"

"Nineteen."

"You go down to Little Bohemia often?"

"Quite a lot."

"Why?"

"I know some people down there. I pal around with some guys."

"All of you with flashlights?"

"No, just me."

"They're not in your social class, these boys you pal around with, are they?"

"Who cares? We have fun."

"Only you're the only one with the flashlight?"

"Well, yes."

"What do you do with that flashlight?"

Smith smiled. "Walk along the beach. Shine it on people. See what they're doing."

"And what are they doing?"

Smith rolled his eyes at the ceiling and grinned. "You'd be surprised."

"All right, surprise me."

"They're playing around, boys and girls. Sometimes it's pretty hot stuff."

"That gives you a kick?"

He gave the chief a secret smile. "I find it amusing."

"These pals of yours do this with you?"

"No. This is my own idea."

"You can get in trouble trying something like that. Some of those people you shine the light on might not like it."

The boy smiled again in his secret way. "Maybe, but the people who like it the least can do the least about it."

A corner of the chief's mouth tightened for a moment and his face became bland again. "How often do you do this sort of thing?"

The boy shrugged. "I don't know. Whenever I feel like it."

"About how often is that, every time the moon gets close to full?"

"No. Nothing like that. You see more interesting things when there's no moon at all as a matter of fact."

"About how often, Smith?"

"Does it matter?"

"It matters."

"Oh, say once or twice a week in the summer. When I happen to be down there and nothing much to do."

"It was twice in two days last week, wasn't it? Friday night and Saturday night?"

"I guess it was."

"What do you do it for?"

Smith shrugged. "Oh, let's say it's an interesting study in human nature. I'm interested in people and how they behave."

"Is it the girls you're interested in or the boys?"

"Both. Both together, that is."

"How about separately? You go out with girls?"

Smith was continuing his smile but a slight wariness crept into his eyes. "Now and then," he said carefully.

"But you'd rather pal around with the boys?"

"Sure. I've got friends of both sexes. Haven't we all?"

"Any boy in particular you pal around with?"

"There're two or three. We go around together."

"What're their names?"

"I told that gentleman their names. Do you want him to write them down again?"

Fellows looked up at Lambert who said, "They're the two I got his name from. Dick Ward and Sam Trevor. They live in a Mrs. Gault's house on Number Two Street."

Fellows returned to the youth. "You ever kiss a girl?"

The boy wasn't smiling now. He was watchful. "Aren't you getting a little personal?"

"Come, come," Fellows said. "I didn't know boys kept that sort of thing secret—not if they *did* it. Maybe if they didn't they wouldn't want to say."

"Oh I've done that."

"How much more?"

The boy flushed a little. "I think that's getting too personal."

"Are girls more fun to kiss than boys or would you say it's the other way around?"

Smith became more offhand. "I really wouldn't know," he said. "I don't kiss boys."

Fellows nodded. "But you do like to see them kiss girls—other boys, that is—and do other things?"

Smith smiled secretly again. "Especially other things."

Fellows leaned forward on his elbows. "What gives you the kick really? Seeing girls with their pants down or is it something else?"

"It's behavior," Smith said, still smiling. "I told you I'm interested in human behavior. I like to observe humans when they don't know they're being observed."

"Their sex behavior, really. Isn't that it?"

The boy passed it off. "Well that's the most interesting aspect of human behavior, after all."

"Well now," Fellows said. "I suppose it is. Let's see, what time did you go out to observe human behavior Saturday night?"

Smith shrugged. He seemed to be enjoying himself. "I don't know. It was when I felt like it."

"What time did you get this feeling?"

"It's not a question of time. I don't know what time."

"Ten thirty, maybe?"

"Oh, maybe."

"You go up to the far end of the beach by any chance?"

"You mean where the murder was?"

"That's what I mean. Your interest in human behavior include an interest in murder?"

"That's human behavior, isn't it?"

Fellows sat back and rested his hands flat on the table. His voice was a little sharper and his eye more calculating. "What do you know about the murder, Gordon?"

"Me?" The lad smiled. "Why should I know anything about it?"

"I should think you'd know something. You were down on that beach with a flashlight shining it on people unexpectedly. A fellow bent on murdering a girl on that beach wouldn't be planning on having a light shined on him. Or, if he'd already done the deed and you were exploring the beach you might shine your light and find nothing but a girl all by herself and you might ask yourself why she's alone. Isn't that right?"

"Well, I suppose I might."

"Was she alone or was she with a boy when you saw her?"

Smith smiled. "I think you're trying to lay a little trap," he said. "But you don't have to play games with me. All you need to do is ask me something and I'll tell you. Trying to outsmart me won't get you anything."

Fellows frowned questioningly. "Was I trying to trap you?"

"If I said, for example, that I found the body, which was what you were really asking me, then you'd want to know why I didn't report it." He smiled. "You see, I find the behavior of policemen interesting too."

"Well, Mr. Smith, I'm pleased to know we're interesting. I've frankly always regarded us policemen as rather of a dull lot myself. But let's get back to the beach. Am I to understand that the girl was not alone when you found her?"

Smith smiled patronizingly. "Haven't you forgotten to ask *if* I found her? That beach is a good quarter of a mile long, you know."

"Pardon me," Fellows said elaborately. "It never occurred to me that you wouldn't walk to the end."

"That's because you don't know much about that beach. I should explain it to you."

Lambert cast a querulous glance at the chief but Fellows was tilting his chair back and saying blandly, "I wish you would."

"Well," Smith said, sitting up more importantly, "the behavior of the couples varies. It follows a pattern but it varies. On dark nights you'll find them grouped closer together, sometimes you'll find two couples within ten feet of each other. When it's a moonlit night they spread out more. Privacy is what they're after and when it's bright they have to be farther away from each other to get it. Then, too, the distance depends on what they're there for. If it's just a few kisses they aren't too fussy. Most of them, though, are interested in more than that." He gave his confidential smile and added, "Sometimes a great deal more."

"Yes," the chief said. "I follow that."

"The next point," Smith said, "is that the human animal is lazy. He doesn't want to go any farther for his privacy than he has to. As a result, you find greater spacing in the area of the pavilion where you can walk extra yards without trouble. Then, about halfway up the beach they bunch more. They're getting lazy about walking and will willingly sacrifice some of the privacy to save walking. And, of course, some people are more interested in privacy than other people.

"Beyond the middle of the beach they begin to thin out and from there on you have what I would call the timid types, those few who want real seclusion for one reason or another. It thins out rapidly and usually by the time you've gone three quarters the length of the beach you run out of people entirely."

Fellows said, "Then you're trying to say you don't bother with that last part of the beach?"

Smith smiled. "One could say the more private the more interesting."

Fellows sat up and his voice sharpened again. "You're fencing, Smith. Either you went all the way up the beach and saw something or you didn't. If you did, I want to hear about it. If you didn't, I don't want to waste my time talking to you."

Smith rolled his eyes. "Well, I have to admit there was a couple at the end of the beach. It was the last couple, in fact."

Fellows' eyes darted keenly. "This was a couple, you say?"

The boy nodded.

"What were they doing?"

Smith considered the question for a moment. "I couldn't tell too well," he said at last. "He was on top of her. That much I know but I couldn't be sure what they were doing."

"You shine your light on them?"

Smith nodded again.

"And what happened?"

"The boy looked around."

"He looked at you? Into the light?"

"That's right."

"What else?"

"Just that. He looked at me until I turned the light off."

"He didn't say anything?"

"No. He just looked."

"What about the girl? What did she do?"

Smith glanced around the room and then looked at the chief conspiratorially. "She didn't do anything. She didn't move."

"How was she lying? Was she dressed?"

Smith shrugged. "I couldn't tell. I couldn't see her very much. Just her feet."

"And how were her feet?"

"Together. The man was straddling her."

This time Fellows glanced at Lambert. "You getting this?"

"The essentials."

He turned back to the youth. "What did this fellow look like?"

"Red hair," Smith answered without hesitation. "Red hair, a rather ugly face, receding chin."

"Red hair?" Fellows said with slight surprise. "What kind of a build?"

"Tall, skinny."

Fellows went on. "Another couple saw this boy with the girl. They said he was dark."

Smith remained unshaken. "I don't know who they think they saw but the man I saw had red hair. Bright red."

Fellows rubbed his chin. "If we took you down to the beach could you show us the exact spot you saw them lying?"

Smith shook his head and smiled patronizingly again. "Oh, no. I'd look like a fool. I couldn't find the exact spot. All I know is that it was near the far end of the beach and they were the last couple."

"You went to the end of the beach looking for more?"

"That's right."

"You couldn't have missed one or two?"

"No. It was light enough so you could see shapes. I could tell where everybody was."

"Where was the couple just preceding the red-haired man?"

"You mean John Carlson and Linda Waters? Nearer the pavilion by about forty yards."

"You read their statements then? You weren't ignorant of the fact a murder was committed? Why did you make us look for you? Why didn't you come in here with this information on your own?"

Smith shrugged and smiled slightly. "*Touché*," he said. "You got me on that one after all." He sat up a little. "Well, the reason is that I didn't really know that was the couple. I heard about the murder and I read some about it but I got so many conflicting reports I didn't really know where it all happened and I didn't want to say anything because I might involve a perfectly innocent man."

Fellows frowned but said nothing more on that. "Would you

know this man again if you saw him? Have you ever seen him before?"

Smith grinned. "The answers are yes and yes."

"You have seen him before? Where?"

"Around Little Bohemia."

"When?"

"I don't remember. Off and on during the summer. I couldn't
tell you what days."

"What was he doing?"

"Nothing in particular. Just walking around on the streets."

Fellows looked up at Lambert. "If he lives there we shouldn't
have any trouble. If he's a summer resident—well, we should be
able to trace him all right." He turned back to the boy. "What
I'd like you to do, son, is go along with Mr. Lambert here and
tour Little Bohemia and see if you spot this man. Will you do
that?"

Smith grinned broadly. "I'd be delighted."

CHAPTER XIII

The Flashlight Kid, in the company of Patrolman Lambert,
didn't spot the redheaded man in question that afternoon but
he did get his picture in the papers. The fact that he had been
found was released by the chief of police but the reporters followed that up on their own. In an interview with Gordon Smith
they learned all about his importance in the case as a material
witness. It took little imagination, in fact, to suggest that the
Flashlight Kid's penchant for surprising lovers on the dark beach
resulted in his catching the murderer in the actual act of strangling his victim.

Fellows sent him out with Lambert again on Thursday to continue the hunt and the youth patrolled the streets of Little Bohemia aware of the attention he attracted, the whispers that circulated along his path and the power he held. A pointed finger and the man at whom he pointed would be arrested. He might even go to the electric chair on the testimony he himself presented in court. Gordon Smith was having opportunities to observe human nature well beyond normal expectancy.

Fellows, meanwhile, stayed in his office going over the meager reports on the case, seeing what he could read into the negative evidence that kept coming in. Despite the intensive hunt through Little Bohemia, no one had been found who remembered seeing Betty and her date between nine o'clock and the time the arm-in-arm couple passed John Carlson and Linda Waters on the beach. It was a disappointing result but it lent weight to the theory Fellows was coming to accept—that the murder was not a spontaneously emotional act but the result of cold premeditation. Fellows was pretty sure the lack of witnesses to Betty's date was no accident. The man she had innocently gone off to meet had deliberately kept her away from public places.

The other theory he held—that Betty's in-laws lived in a nearby town—he was ready to abandon, however. All the Moores in all the towns in Pittsfield County, as well as a number in neighboring counties, had been checked out by the local police forces and none could be shown to have had any connection with the dead girl whatever.

This unexpected development had the chief baffled for it left unanswered the question of how Betty had learned about Little Bohemia, how she had happened to come there and where she had come from. Though reason told him the police investigations had been thorough and though, intellectually, he gave up the idea of the Moores living close by, emotionally he couldn't quite shake the idea that Betty hadn't come from far away.

There were other problems that begged for answers. In what state, since it wasn't Connecticut, had Henry Moore been killed? Just where did his family live and why had they not come forward and admitted the relationship?

At noon County Coroner Clement Avery called up and loaded the chief's shoulders with his own problems. "Here it is, Thursday," he complained, "and you don't know a damned thing. I have to call an inquest but there's no point in an inquest unless there's something to point to at it. You don't even know who the girl is, let alone who killed her. What the hell am I supposed to do?"

Fellows patiently explained his own difficulties and the work that was being done. "Wilks is organizing a check of shipping lists and we've wired Washington for passport information."

"And how long before anything comes out of that, if ever? God knows when she sailed, if she ever *did* sail."

"I think she sailed all right, Clem. There's the sticker on her suitcase and the seasick pills. And it might not take long to find out about it. The passport information we should have pretty soon. As for when she sailed, I kind of think it would have been within the last three months, after her husband was killed. She takes a little trip by herself to get over it, goes back to her in-laws, gets hung up there, and comes here. I kind of doubt she'd have spent the whole three months with her in-laws. If she's going to feel the need to get away at all she's going to feel it pretty quickly, I think."

Avery grumbled some more and said that he'd decided to hold the inquest the following Tuesday, come hell or high water, "and, for God's sake, try to have something for me by then."

Sid Wilks called up at three that afternoon to report that operation "passenger list" was ready to go and Lerner and Daniels could come to New York and take it over. "It's not going to be any cinch," he said. "You any idea how many ships come in and out of New York? Everything from freighters with a dozen passengers to the big liners with two thousand. They come from everywhere and they go everywhere, Europe, the Orient, South America, the Caribbean, the Mediterranean, every place but the north and south poles."

The New York police had assigned a detective to help and

work was already started, he said. They'd searched the records back to August fifteenth so far. "Meanwhile," Wilks went on, "who's this 'Flashlight Kid' I'm reading about? What's he got, really?"

"He's a strange one," Fellows told him. "He gives me the willies."

"Just so long as he doesn't give you the runaround. Did he see the murder or did he do the murder?"

"I have no idea. I've got nothing that says he did it and, as a matter of fact, nothing but his statement that he saw it. I checked with the couple that heard the girl cry 'No. No.' this morning and they swore nobody shined any flashlight on them while they were out on the beach and they don't remember any single man walking by them, though they couldn't be certain about that."

"But he went through Little Bohemia yesterday afternoon and didn't find his redheaded man?"

"That's right, and he's continuing the search today."

"How long does it take to go through that place? He sounds like a headline hunter to me."

"He sounds sick if you want to know how I feel about it but that doesn't mean he couldn't have seen something. It also doesn't mean he couldn't have done something too. We're assuming the man Mrs. Moore had the date with strangled her but it's possible he left her for some reason and this kid or somebody else came along and found her alone. It doesn't matter, though, we still have to go along with this kid and let him hunt for the redheaded man. I put Lambert with him and I gave Lambert instructions to watch him carefully and report on his behavior. The kid might give himself away and Lambert's savvy enough to pick it up."

"I wish I was around to go with him. Anybody who gets his kicks spying on neckers—there's something wrong with him. I'd like to know just how wrong he is."

"Relax. I wasn't born yesterday."

"Neither was I and I have a hunch there's no such person as a redheaded man."

"I've thought of that too but we still have to find out."

The answer to this question was one of the few Fellows received before he expected it. At half past three, when the first of the four o'clock shift was starting to arrive and Fellows was out at the main desk checking assignments on his clipboard, the door opened suddenly and the man who came in brought everyone up in surprise. He was lean, angular and scowling. He had a face full of freckles, a receding chin and flaming red hair. He stood for a moment, picking out the chief, and then came forward. "What's all this about me and that dead girl?" he demanded.

CHAPTER XIV

Fellows recovered himself almost immediately and a corner of his mouth twisted faintly. "Well," he said. "We've been looking for you."

"So I gather," the redheaded man retorted bitterly. "It's in all the papers and I know my description when I see it and when I get hold of that flashlight-shining bastard again, even his mother won't know him."

Fellows moved closer, to a position slightly behind the man. He gestured at the door and said, "Come on in the office and relax. By the way, I didn't get your name." His tone was kindly but the position he'd taken left the youth little alternative.

"Allen Bacon's my name," the redhead said, the bitterness still in his voice. "And I want to know just what's going on."

Fellows guided him to the office and said over his shoulder to Unger, "Take over the inspection. And put out a call for Lambert and the boy. Get them in here as fast as you can."

He closed the door and pulled out a chair for Bacon. "Just make yourself comfortable," he said and took his own, tilting it back.

Bacon sat stiffly. He was wearing khaki pants and an open shirt which showed red fuzz on his chest. He pushed a freckled hand through his hair and said, "I don't get all this."

"It's easy," Fellows told him. "This boy with the flashlight thinks he saw somebody on the beach with the girl who was killed. The description rather fits you as a matter of fact."

"It *is* me," Bacon said. "That's what I'm here about. I wasn't on that beach Saturday night with the dead girl or any other girl. I was at a show and the girl I was with will back me up. That guy's a god—I mean he's an out-and-out liar. He's trying to stick this on me because I busted him one in the nose. Him and his god—I mean him going around shining that flashlight on people, scaring the hell out of them like he might be a cop or something. He had it coming to him and now he's trying to frame me for murdering a girl I never heard of." The man leaned forward, pale and plaintive. "I mean what's wrong with him?"

Fellows opened his hands. "I don't know, son. I just sit around and ask questions and hope the answers I get are honest."

"Well his aren't, not if he's trying to claim I'm the one he saw. I was never there and I've got a witness to prove it. I never knew this girl who got killed. I never heard of her. I was never around the beach last Saturday night. I was in the movies here in town."

Fellows sat up and sorted through the stuff on his desk and in a drawer for a blank piece of paper and a pencil. "I might as well take down the name of your witness, just to be formal about it. And her address and your address."

The youth's white skin went whiter still under the freckles. "Are you arresting me?"

"No, no," Fellows said offhandedly, waving the pencil. "This is just routine. We always take names and addresses. They're always the first two questions we ask. We collect names and addresses. We've got books full of them."

Bacon gave the girl's name as Natalie Dwyer. She lived in the Crestwood section of Stockford as did he. "You see what a liar that Smith is?" he said. "Suggesting I live in Little Bohemia. I live way the other side of town."

"He has been rather looking for you in the wrong place," Fellows admitted. "That is if it's you he's looking for. You punched him, eh? For shining a light on you down on the beach?"

"That's right. Back two or three weeks ago. I forget what day."

"And you think he's trying to get even?"

"That's the only thing I can think of because why else would he say he saw me with the dead girl when I was at the movies with Natalie? There can't be two people with a face like mine."

"You any objection to letting him look at you and see what he says?"

"No."

"Good, because I'm having him brought in. If you're right and his description was to get even it's a rather strange way of doing it."

"Anybody who'd go around with a flashlight like him is strange to start with. It wouldn't surprise me if he did the job himself."

Fellows sat back and smiled. "And are you now trying to get even with him?"

Bacon flushed but said nothing.

The chief got out his chewing tobacco and allowed the boy to smoke. He asked more questions and learned that Bacon worked in a dairy six days a week and that Thursday was his day off. He'd been violently upset when he read the papers and had been in a quandary what to do. He didn't confide in his mother, with whom he lived, but finally called up Natalie where she worked and she was the one who advised that he go to the police. "She thought it would look better," he said lamely, staring at the table.

"It's the smartest thing you could have done," Fellows told him. "She's right about the kind of impression it makes. As long as she says you were with her at the movies when the murder was committed I don't see that you have anything to worry about."

"I've got to worry about that crackpot Smith, don't I? I never even knew his name till I saw it and his picture in the paper. When I saw the picture I knew who he was right off. It was dark when I busted him. We had a little tussle and he tried to bean me with that flashlight but I hauled off and bashed him a good right to the nose and he went down. He was blubbering about bleeding and then he got up and ran. You should have heard the shriek he let out when I hit him, too. It sounded like a woman, I swear."

"And you're certain it's the same boy?"

"Absolutely. Like I say, it was dark and I couldn't see his face too good but I got the feel of him. It's hard to say what I mean but he was soft and weak like and when I saw that face in the paper, I knew it right off. Same kind of heavy soft face and narrow eyes. I recognized his picture even before I read who he was. And then I read what he said about me and how the cops were looking for me and I don't mind telling you I got scared." He hesitated. "You're sure I'm doing the right thing coming in like this?"

Fellows nodded. "Was it Natalie you were on the beach with? Would she verify that you punched him?"

"That wasn't Natalie. That was another girl. But she would. I'm sure of it."

The four o'clock shift had gone out on duty by the time Lambert came in with young Gordon Smith. When Unger rapped on the door and said they were outside, Fellows left Bacon where he was and went out to meet them. "Any luck?" he asked, looking at Smith rather than Lambert.

"Not yet, Chief."

"I've got a man inside I'd like you to take a look at. He might be the one."

Smith covered his surprise well, but not completely. "Why sure," he said.

"Mr. Bacon, would you come out please?"

Bacon came to the door and Fellows' eyes were on the Flashlight Kid. The youth's expression flickered and when Bacon said, "You son of a bitch," he shrank back noticeably.

Fellows said, "This man is Mr. Bacon, Smith. He look familiar?"

Smith debated, not moving his gaze from the man's face. Finally he made a slight negative motion with his head. "No, that's not the man."

"Red hair, you said, Smith. Tall and thin. He fits the description."

"Yes, but he's—I didn't see him in Little Bohemia," Smith said, still staring.

"What's that got to do with it?" Fellows said with an edge to his voice.

Smith turned then to the chief. "I mean he resembles him some but it's not the same man. I can tell. It's not the same man I saw."

"Who you saw that night? That what you mean?"

"That's right. Who I saw that night."

"But you've seen Mr. Bacon before. That's right, isn't it?"

Smith shook his head vigorously. "No. I never saw him before in my life."

There was contempt on Fellows' face. He turned. "Well, Mr. Bacon, it seems that Mr. Smith here doesn't recognize you after all. I guess there's no need to stay around any longer. Thanks for coming in."

Bacon walked out jauntily and Smith bit his lip watching him. When the outside door closed he turned to Lambert and Fellows. "Uh, do I go back again?"

"Not right away," Fellows told him. "We're going to have a little talk first. You and Mr. Lambert and me."

They brought him into the office and put him in Bacon's chair. Lambert stood by the door again and the chief sat at the desk. "Well, John," Fellows said to the patrolman. "You've been with him. What do you think?"

Lambert regarded the youth with no great love but he only shrugged. "I don't think he saw what he says he saw. I think he's a liar myself. I don't know what else he might be."

Fellows turned to the boy. "You hear what Mr. Lambert said, Smith? You going to defend yourself?"

"He doesn't know what he's talking about," Smith said sullenly. "I know what I saw."

"You said you saw a redheaded man but when we show him to you you change your mind. Why, Smith?"

"I did see a redheaded man. It wasn't him though."

"His twin brother?"

"It was another redheaded man."

Fellows sat up. "Do you know what happens to people who deliberately try to mislead the police, Smith?"

"I wasn't trying to mislead you."

"You denied ever seeing that man before, didn't you? You said you never laid eyes on him. You don't want us to know he punched you in the nose for shining a flashlight on him down on the beach a couple of weeks ago. Why did you lie about that, Smith?"

Smith was flustered. "He's the liar," he said. "He never punched me."

"Describe the man who punched you then. You shined the light on him. You saw what he looked like."

"It wasn't him," Smith said steadfastly.

"Describe who it was."

"I don't remember too well."

"You don't remember too well? You don't remember the man you shined your light on who punched you? But you can describe the man at the end of the beach, one man among the dozens you shined your light on?"

"He was murdering the girl."

"You *knew* he was murdering the girl when you shined your light on him?"

"No, no. But I noticed she was quiet. That's why I remember."

Fellows' face was tight and his teeth clenched. "You never shined your light on that couple at the end of the beach, Smith. We've got testimony from the next couple over. That doesn't mean you weren't there at the end of the beach, though. But this was one time you weren't using your light. Why weren't you using it, Smith? Was that girl alone when you found her? What did you do to her and why?"

Smith said, "You're crazy. I never did anything to her. I don't know what you're talking about. It was a redheaded man."

"It was a redheaded man who punched you, Smith. Why are you trying to involve him in the murder?"

"I'm not," Smith protested. "Didn't I tell you he wasn't the one?"

"Where were you at eleven o'clock last Saturday, Smith? Who were you with? What witnesses have you got to say where you were?"

Smith's usually veiled eyes widened and became clear. "I was —I don't remember where I was."

"You were around that girl, weren't you?"

"I didn't know that girl."

"You were around her. That's where you said you were, isn't that right?"

"I saw the man who was with her."

"There was no redheaded man with her, Smith. The man she was with had dark hair. You lied about that, Smith. Why? Is it because the dark-haired man had left her when you came along and there was nobody with her when you found her and you had to make it up about somebody being with her to cover yourself so you made it up about the redheaded man who punched you? That's what you did, didn't you? You made it up about the redheaded man to cover yourself." He sat forward. "Come on, Smith. It's not going to do any good holding back. Get it off your chest. That's what happened, isn't it?"

"No. That's not it at all."

"She was a very beautiful girl, wasn't she, Smith? And all alone on the beach. Did she beckon to you? Tell us what she did, Smith. Maybe you couldn't resist her. A beautiful girl like that. Was she a willing girl, Smith?"

Smith said frantically, "I wasn't there. I didn't see her. I swear I never saw her."

"You wouldn't miss the end of the beach when you went around with your little flashlight. You know you wouldn't.

That's where all the most interesting studies of human nature would be, wouldn't they? Tell us what happened down there. You wanted to do a little personal experimenting, didn't you?"

"You're crazy. I didn't go anywhere near there," Smith said and looked ready to cry.

"Of course you went there. You told us you did. You were down there at the end of the beach at eleven o'clock Saturday night. You admitted it."

"No. That's not true."

"You ever been to a psychiatrist, Smith?"

"No."

"You're just a little mixed up. You're interested in human behavior. You like to study people, don't you? It wasn't very nice of you to try to blame the redheaded man for killing the girl when all he did was punch you in the nose, now, was it? Do you think that was a nice thing to do?"

"No," he said, half sobbing.

"You should have told us the truth, Smith. You should have told us there was nobody with that girl, shouldn't you?"

"I wasn't there," he wailed. "I didn't even go on the beach till midnight."

"Now that's not so, Smith. You know that's not so. Why you told us yourself you were on the beach at eleven o'clock. Not only on the beach but way at the far end. That's where you were, wasn't it?"

"No," he cried. "I didn't go down there till midnight." He dug his fists in his eyes and said, "I want to go home now."

"You can't go home, Smith. You're a material witness. We need you. You're the only one who saw the girl when she was being murdered. Do you realize that? The only one. That's why we need you. We need you to tell us how she was murdered. You're going to do that for us, aren't you?"

"I told you I wasn't there."

"Now you tell us that, but yesterday afternoon about this time you told us you were there. I told you you shouldn't try to mislead the police and here you are trying to do it. We're not going to let you, Smith. We're going to keep you here till you tell us about how she was murdered."

"I was never there," he pleaded desperately. "I didn't go on the beach till midnight, till way after she was murdered. I was somewhere else. I was with some guys. I was with Dick Ward and Sammy Trevor."

"We know about those boys you hang out with, Smith. They didn't say anything about being with you Saturday. Not one thing."

"They're trying to protect themselves. That's why. They're lying. We were at Ward's place looking at some dirty movies he's got. That's why I went down there that night."

"So you saw dirty movies that night?"

"That's right. That's where I was and they're trying to get me in trouble protecting their own skins." His voice came up in a half shriek. "I was *there!*"

"And that gave you ideas, didn't it? You saw those dirty movies and then you went out looking for a girl."

"No. I didn't go out on the beach till midnight."

"You went on the beach at midnight? All right, let's say it was midnight. And you walked the length of the beach shining your little flashlight so you could study human behavior and when you reached the end of the beach there was this girl."

"No. I told you it was after the girl was murdered."

"It was after the girl was murdered. She was dead. She was lying on the sand, dead, and you found her."

"No," he screamed. "I never went to the end of the beach. I never found her at all."

"Stop trying to tell us you didn't go to the end of the beach. You always go to the end of the beach. You don't want to miss anything."

"Not that night. Not that night, I tell you. A guy chased me. I ran back. That's all that happened. I didn't even go half way."

"Who chased you, a redheaded guy with a receding chin?"

Gordon Smith didn't answer. He put his head down on the table and sobbed.

CHAPTER XV

The Flashlight Kid wasn't held for murder but he was held for psychiatric examination. As Fellows said to Wilks when the detective sergeant returned from New York, "He's capable. I think he could be capable of anything. But whether he *did* anything or not is something else again."

The chief's personal view was that Gordon Smith had *not* done anything—except lie to the police. To him, a boy who got his kicks spying on other people making love lacked what it took to do it on his own. He further believed that Smith had never stumbled on the body at all. If he had, he would likely have panicked and, in any event, he wouldn't have kept quiet about it. The Flashlight Kid liked headlines too much.

Despite this view, Fellows was thorough in his investigation of the boy. He had his room searched for anything that belonged to Betty Moore and he led a small raid in Little Bohemia on the rooms of Dick Ward and Sam Trevor. The search of Smith's home produced nothing and the raid little more. Three reels of pornographic movies were uncovered in a paper bag on a closet shelf and the boys were arrested on that count despite their claims they didn't know what was in the bag and were keeping it for a friend. At headquarters they refused to alibi Gordon Smith but this meant little. The two "creeps" as Wilks termed them, were shabby and shaggy and their word didn't seem any more reliable than Smith's had been. Their refusal to alibi him was more likely revenge or an effort to save their own skins than truth and Fellows was convinced by Friday night that the Flashlight Kid episode was nothing but a diversion in the case of Elizabeth Moore.

Those aspects which were related to the case, however, produced no more than the diversion had. Information came in from Washington on Friday and included a list of fourteen Elizabeth Moores with American passports and whose age range and other data fit the dead girl. By Tuesday morning the list had been processed and all fourteen were found to be alive and well.

By Tuesday morning, also, the motor vehicle departments of twenty-eight states, including all those in the east, had reported no automobile fatalities involving the girl's husband. A grim Fred Fellows had nothing whatever to give Clement Avery when the County Coroner came down for the inquest that afternoon.

The inquest, held in the Stockford Town Hall at two P.M. was, as a result, entirely negative in character. Psychiatric examination of Gordon Smith indicated that while he was further from the norm than the average man, he could not be termed abnormal, let alone irrational, and it was the concensus of the doctors who tested him that he had had no contact with the girl on the beach. His original statements to the contrary were interpreted as an effort to feed an ego admittedly immense.

The rest of the testimony was nothing but a rehash of what was now the public history of the case. Chief Fellows told of the futile attempt to locate the girl's in-laws. Other patrolmen related their failure to learn whom the girl had been with on the fatal night.

Mrs. Fremont testified as to the background the girl had given her and the letter that had come. John Carlson and Linda Waters told of the couple who had passed by arm-in-arm to a farther spot on the beach and how they had heard the girl cry out, "No. No."

It was a short inquest, poorly attended and devoid of surprises. At its conclusion Avery gave the only verdict possible: "Death of a girl called Elizabeth Moore by strangling at the hands of a man unknown."

As soon as it was over the coroner stalked out of the hearing room on the second floor and let off steam to Fellows and Wilks in the police chief's office. "What kind of a turn-out do you call that?" he raged. "There wasn't a single newspaper reporter in the crowd. Not even the guy from your local weekly was there."

"Carleton Lawrence?" Fellows answered. "He goes to press today. He'd be over at the newsshop putting the paper together. As for the other papers, I expect the reporters will call in to get the story."

"That's fine coverage, I will say. There hasn't been a word about the case since Saturday."

"There hasn't been anything to write about since Saturday, Clem. As for the inquest, Lawrence saw no point holding off his deadline to cover it. He wrote a short piece about it in advance and all he needs is the actual wording of your verdict."

"What about the psychiatrists who testified? Nobody knew what *they* were going to say."

"Carl did. He called them this morning."

Avery made a face. "This whole thing stinks. Nothing's being done. The guy's getting away with murder."

Fellows said drily, "Thanks for the compliment."

"Well, what about it?" Avery retorted testily. "You don't really expect to get anything from pawn shops about her watch, do you? And what about all those motor vehicle departments who were going to help so much? You've heard from over half of them and there's no Henry Moore."

"There're twenty states left, Clem, within the continental limits anyway. We'll get a break there pretty soon. And there're the passenger lists. It takes a long time to go through those but there's no question about her going on a ship and pretty soon we'll find out which one."

"Just the way you were going to find out about her passport, I suppose."

Fellows shrugged. "I'm sorry about that, but it reminds me of a little story. There were two guys prospecting for oil out around the edge of a big desert out west and you know what? Every place they dug they struck water instead. They got so fed up with that that they moved far away from where they were hitting all that water, way out into the middle of the desert and there they drilled again. Well, this time they really got a gusher. Oil came out of there by the tankcarful.

"Now you'd think that's a story with a happy ending, but it isn't. You know why? Because they were so far out in the desert they died of thirst."

Avery gave Fellows a dim look. "What's that got to do with passports?"

"Well, the moral of the story is that sometimes the stuff you think you don't want can do you some good after all. Like the passports. I admit it's a disappointment that we couldn't find an application for this particular Elizabeth Moore but it has its bright side too. We know she couldn't have taken a ship to any foreign port where a passport is required and that's going to save us a lot of time. All we have to look at now are incoming ships, just in case she's a foreigner, and those outgoing ships that are cruise ships or are sailing to American territories or possessions. We should track her down pretty fast now."

Avery grumbled and muttered and even suggested—no reflection on the chief, of course—that maybe the State Police should handle the investigation. Then he left with Fellows seeing him to the door.

"He's very flattering today," Wilks said sourly when the chief came back. "He'd charm the hide off an elephant."

Fellows was philosophical. "Don't mind him, Sid. He's peeved over the lack of publicity. You know coroners. A hot case like this and by the time he gets into it it's stone cold dead." He shrugged. "Personally, I've got no kick on that score. At least we're spared long editorials about police inefficiency and how it's time to put me out to pasture. We don't have crowds pounding on the door in a panic because people can get away with murder on our beaches. If it'd been earlier, before the season ended, we might have."

"What you're saying," Wilks said stonily, "is that nobody gives a damn. A girl gets murdered. A very beautiful girl. A girl a man wouldn't mind having for his own daughter, and nobody pays any attention. Nobody cares who she was or where she came from. Nobody even seems to care that it might happen again."

"I suppose," Fellows said, sitting down heavily, "that's because she doesn't come from around here. People have been convinced by the papers that her death was due to something in her past and not due to the beach at Indian Lake."

"Yeah. As long as she's not from around here we can forget about her. As long as she doesn't involve us, we don't care."

"You care," Fellows said. "You seem to care a great deal."

Wilks said bitterly, "She was pretty and young and nice."

"And you wouldn't mind having a girl like her for a daughter."

"We could have. Marge and I've been married long enough. Anyway, I don't like things like that happening to a young kid like her. I'm like Dzanowski. 'I break his neck.'"

Fellows smiled. "I know," he said. "I see a girl like her killed like that and it makes me wonder what kind of boys my daughters are going out with and what they do together. My boys I don't worry about but I'll be glad when the girls are married and settled down."

Wilks nodded and bit off some chewing tobacco. "The trouble is I don't like the waiting. There's nothing we can get our teeth into. We've got to sit while twenty more states report on auto accidents. We've got to wait while Ed and Lerner and Daniels and the New York detective working with them wade through passenger lists."

"So we wait," Fellows said. "And pretty soon one or both of those leads will hit pay-dirt and things will come to life again. It's just time."

"Is it? That's what's starting to bother me. All the states in the east have reported and there's no Henry Moore. It seems to me he should have had his accident somewhere in this half of the country. And those passenger lists. They're working on June now. And here we've been figuring she took her sea voyage *after* her husband was killed and only just before she came here."

Fellows shrugged. "Well, it's starting to look as though she took the trip before he was killed. There's nothing wrong with that."

"Unless she didn't sail from New York, or unless Lewis

missed a name somewhere on a passenger list. Maybe I ought
to go down there again."

"Ed's doing the job, Sid. Relax. We'll get a break any day
now."

CHAPTER XVI

Fred Fellows' optimism waned as the days passed. His expected
break did not arrive and what little passed his desk was bad
news. Ed Lewis phoned daily with a progress report but all that
ever consisted of was how far back they'd gone in New York
shipping. By the seventeenth of September, a week after the
inquest and almost two weeks after the burial, they had processed lists back through late April. Meanwhile, state after state
reported no fatalities involving a Henry Moore.

Activities at Stockford Police Headquarters had long since
returned to normal and the only variation in routine was the
shifting of schedules due to Lerner's and Daniels' assignment
to the passenger lists. Even Fellows and Wilks seldom mentioned the case any more. Other problems in a town of 8000
loomed in their lives as policemen and held their attention. Until
Ed Lewis stumbled on the right Mrs. Moore or some state reported the accident they sought or some pawnshop turned up
the diamond studded wristwatch there was nowhere to go and
no place to look.

The case was not forgotten, however, and if it was no longer
a subject of conversation it remained in the back of every policeman's mind. There was less joking among the men, less of the
easy interplay. A picture of the girl, the best of Ecklund's por-
traits, stared from the bulletin board where Dzanowski had

tacked it and she smiled out at all the men as if to say, "Please remember what was done to me."

For the others there was little to do but remember. Fellows, however, bore the responsibility for the case and he grew daily grimmer with frustration at the waiting and at the lack of success. He took the case file home with him Monday night and Tuesday was almost the first day-off in memory that he didn't put in at least one appearance at headquarters to check on things.

Tuesday night he came out of hiding and took himself down the cellar stairs of Sid Wilks' house to where the detective sergeant had his model trains. Wilks was running an engine he had constructed around the tracks when Fellows ducked under the electric light bulb at the foot of the stairs and came across the floor. "How do you like that baby?" Wilks said, gesturing with pride at the lone circling engine. "Isn't she a beaut?"

"Yeah. It beats walking."

Wilks shut off the transformer and turned around. "Don't tell me. This is a business visit and it has to do with Betty Moore and it doesn't have to do with some state reporting her husband being killed." He grinned. "How did I do?"

"You get three stars for that. They'll make you a captain yet."

"I further deduce, since we didn't see your shining face around headquarters today, that you've been sweating over the case and have come up with something. I'll guess it has to do with what conclusions you'll draw if all the continental states give you a negative answer."

"That's part of it."

"I think you're going to get that negative answer too, Fred."

"So do I."

"So what's the conclusion, that it was Hawaii or Alaska, or a foreign country? I'll take a foreign country myself."

"I'll go you one better. I don't think he was killed at all."

Wilks arched an eyebrow at the chief. "Well, that's a wrinkle."

"Furthermore," Fellows went on, "I don't think there's any

amorous best man writing letters from Pittsfield. I don't even
think her name is Elizabeth Moore."

"You mean Mrs. Fremont lied to us?"

"I mean the girl lied to Mrs. Fremont. The more I've gone over
this thing the more I'm convinced her whole story is nothing
but a pack of lies. She's no widow. She's probably not even
married."

"Well," Wilks said. "That's certainly an angle."

"You don't like it?"

"No, I don't."

"Why not?"

For answer, Wilks said, "Wait here," and went up the cellar
steps. He was gone two minutes and came back with a manila
envelope from which he withdrew a print of Betty's portrait
photo. He laid it on the train table under the fluorescent light
and pointed. "That's why."

Fellows looked at Wilks. "Say what do you do, keep a copy
of her picture home here?"

"My pin-up girl," Wilks said offhandedly. "I told you I think
she's a sweet kid. Well this is to remind me not to forget we
haven't caught the man who killed her. Like Dzanowski's picture on the bulletin board. Now take a look at that picture.
Look at that girl's face. Does she look like a liar? Be honest now,
Fred."

Fellows gave the picture a passing glance and said, "You can't
tell about things like that. Some of the deadliest murderers look
like the guy next door."

"The deadliest murderers *are* the guys next door. I don't claim
to be any expert but you can size people up pretty well just by
looking at them. As I look at her, she doesn't hit me as the type
of girl who'd go around telling lies. Besides, why would she?"

"How would I know?"

"Well, damn it, if you think she's lying you must have a reason. Mrs. Fremont didn't think she'd lie. You didn't think she'd
lie. Now you do. Something put the bug in your ear."

"I think so because nothing she's told us fits. Where's her dead husband, for instance? Where's that auto accident he's supposed to have had?"

"Because it didn't happen in the United States of America doesn't mean it didn't happen. It might have been in Europe."

Fellows leaned a hand on the train table. "Let's look at it this way, Sid. She's been widowed three months. She'd been very much in love with her husband. She's been on a sea voyage. She didn't make this voyage after her husband died so it must have been before. Then they made the trip together. Now, if she didn't land in this country *after* she was widowed, then he must have been killed here."

"Or Mexico or Canada. You haven't checked those places. She's a girl who traveled a lot."

"You're reaching, don't you think? Let's take a few more things. After this husband she's so much in love with dies, she lives with his folks. She leaves them and the amorous best man to come to Little Bohemia, a patch of land at the end of a lake a mile long and maybe three quarters of a mile wide. It's a resort area primarily for the local gentry. There're no brochures. It's an unheard of place, yet she goes there by bus with a suitcase, not only knowing about it but fully expecting to be able to rent a room without a previous reservation. That means she not only knew about Little Bohemia but she knew enough about the setup to be dead sure she wouldn't find the place booked solid. But her in-laws who, incidentally, have never been heard from, don't live around here."

Wilks shrugged at that. "Who's to say she hadn't been there before, vacationed sometime? That doesn't prove anything."

"All right, let's look at some more things that don't fit. There're those in-laws who've never come forward. If her story was true, why didn't they? Let's go further. She comes to Mrs. Fremont's to get away from in-laws and a man she's leery of. That's the tale she told Mrs. Fremont but nothing she did there makes any sense with regard to what she said. She gets a letter from Pittsfield. This excites her. Mrs. Fremont interpreted it as fright but it could have been pleasure. But if she wanted

to get away from everybody, who knew where to write her? Who
did she give her address to? Wouldn't she have had to have done
it after she rented the room? If so, she wrote a letter or made a
phone call. But is that the action you'd expect from a girl who
wanted to be alone?

"Next, she has a date. This is the girl mourning her husband.
We don't know who the date was with but why would she date
anybody?"

Wilks picked up the picture and gazed at it idly. "Her date
killed her, Fred. The cord, as you pointed out, makes it look premeditated. She told Mrs. Fremont she was afraid of a man.
Obviously she had reason to be. That means she was telling
the truth."

"Was she? She went out with him, didn't she? She got into her
prettiest dress for that date. Nobody was twisting her arm to
make her go out. She was looking forward to her date. That's
not a girl afraid of a man. She should have been, as it turned out,
but she certainly didn't know it."

Wilks sighed and put the picture away from him. "All right.
You're convinced she wasn't telling the truth. What do you
think the truth is?"

Fellows made a face. "That's the trouble. I don't know. I
thought for a bit she might have been trying to break away from
a too-strict family, changing her name so she could kick up her
heels. I even thought the family might have turned their back on
her and so never acknowledged her death, but that doesn't fit her
behavior either. I'm still stumped on that."

"So," Wilks challenged, "even though you don't believe her
story you don't have a better one. Is that it?"

"I'm trying to think of a better one, Sid, because I don't like
the one she told. Let's forget the dead husband. If she had a husband, he's probably not dead."

"If she had a husband why hasn't he come forward? Even if
she changed her name, her picture's been published enough. If
he's alive, why hasn't he at least reported her missing?"

Fellows snorted. "Because if she had a husband, who's the
most likely murderer? Who else would she permit to make love

to her on a beach? Who would be more likely to kill her after the love act and then strip her jewels from her body?"

"So," Wilks said, "you think the supposedly dead husband is the real murderer?"

"I didn't say that. But if she's married, I certainly want to know about the husband. What I really do is question that she had a husband at all."

"The wedding ring was a blind, huh? You mean she was coming down here on some lover's advice, escaping from her family for a big deal with him?"

"That's one of the better possibilities."

"And she waits around for him for ten days? A pretty patient girl, I must say. What's tying him up? Business?"

"Maybe. The 'business' would be another woman, of course."

"And then he writes that he'll see her Saturday? He meets her. Maybe he's parked in the parking lot and they sit in his car. Maybe they go down to the boat docks in Little Bohemia where nobody'll see them. They talk or whatever they do for a couple of hours. He wants to break it off and she won't let him. He wants to get rid of her—kill her—but the dock isn't good because she'd be heard if she screamed and the car isn't good since it's his car. So he takes her to the beach where he can lull her into false security by making love and then choke her." Wilks scoffed. "All very neat except for about three dozen things. Why would she pretend to have a dead husband? Why would the guy pick the beach instead of some private place and why would killing her be the only way out?"

"Don't look at me," Fellows answered. "That's your story, not mine. I don't have any story. I just don't believe hers."

Wilks turned to the picture, shook his head slowly, and said to it, "I'm telling you, Honey-chile, I hope the old man's wrong about you. Because if he isn't and all that you said was a passel of lies, the guy who did you wrong may never have to pay."

Fellows nodded grimly. "That's what's bothering me," he said. "I'm going to keep Ed looking through the passenger lists because that's all we've got left to do but I'm willing to bet she didn't travel as Mrs. Elizabeth Moore. She's a fraud, Sid. I'll lay odds on it. And if I'm right, we're cooked."

Wilks picked up the picture and prepared to slip it back into the envelope. "Well, I'll tell you, Fred. I'd take your odds except that I'm not fool enough to bet on females." He shook his head at the girl's pretty face. "Women! Misguided, misunderstood, misunderstanding. What the hell goes on in your minds?"

CHAPTER XVII

The clock on the wall in the cramped office where Stockford plainclothesman Edward Lewis worked, was approaching ten as he drew the next passenger list over in front of him. The date was Wednesday, September twenty-fifth but the date on the list said February twelfth. This one was for the Dutch liner *Alkmaar* which sailed from Hoboken on a two-week's Caribbean cruise.

Lewis stretched, lighted a cigarette, and turned the pages to the "M" listings. He ran a finger down the column with the practiced speed of one who had done this nearly eight hours a day for eighteen days. There was a Mr. and Mrs. Henry Moore on board. The first name "Henry" was more promising than some of the first names of Moores he'd had to check out but it gave him no particular elation. Nearly every passenger list had at least one "Moore" on its roster and one such list had had five, two of them Henrys. It wasn't skimming-through passenger lists, it was checking out the Moores that took the time, that made the work progress so slowly.

Lewis folded back the sheets and held them with a paperweight. The home address of this Mr. and Mrs. Moore was a small New York hotel and Lewis didn't care much for the sound of that. He took the Manhattan phone book from the bottom drawer of the desk and hunted up the number.

As he went to dial, the light under the button connecting his line went on and David Lerner, one of the other three men in the room, spun his own dial, bent over his passenger list and said into the phone, "Operator, I want to put in a person to person call to Mrs. Eric Moore on Sunset Street in Boulder, Colorado."

Lewis pressed another button opening another line, lifted his phone and dialed the hotel number. When a man gave the name of the hotel and said, "Reception desk," Lewis said, "This is the police department, Lewis speaking. Do you have a Mr. and Mrs. Henry Moore registered there?"

"One moment," the man said and there was the sound of his breathing into the phone as he riffled through cards. "No, sir. No one by that name."

Lewis was afraid of that. The really difficult ones were the Moores who had moved. "All right," he said. "Can you tell me if a Mr. and Mrs. Henry Moore were registered there prior to February twelfth?"

"February twelfth?" the man said. "You mean last February?"

"That's right. Last February."

There was a slight hesitation. "And you said you were?"

"Edward Lewis. Patrolman connected with the New York Police Department."

"I will check for you," the man said sadly.

Lewis picked up his cigarette and sat back for the wait. Across from him Lerner was saying, "Mrs. Moore? You are Mrs. Eric Moore? . . . This is David Lerner of the New York Police Department calling, Mrs. Moore. I would like to ask you a few questions if I may. First. Is it true that you sailed on a Mediterranean cruise last February with your husband? . . . Thank you. Now, can you recall the date of sailing and the name of the ship? . . . Thank you . . . No, this isn't a joke, Mrs. Moore. This is official police business. I wouldn't be calling you all the way from New York as a joke, I can assure you. One more question, please.

Can you give me the names of some of the other passengers who sailed with you?" There was a pause of a minute during which time Lérner turned pages of his list back and forth rapidly. At length he said, "Thank you very much, Mrs. Moore. You've been most helpful . . . I'm sorry, I'm not at liberty to tell you what it's all about. Thank you very much." He hung up, found his place on the list and picked up the phone to call the next Moore.

The receptionist came back on Lewis' line and said, "Yes. We had a Mr. and Mrs. Henry Moore staying with us. They registered on the twenty-ninth of January and checked out the morning of the twelfth of February. Room 1468."

"Did they leave a forwarding address?"

"No, sir. They did not."

"Where did they register from?"

"They put down 'Pennsylvania'."

"Is that all? You don't require a complete address?"

"What's the point of requiring it? Anybody who didn't want to give his real address would make one up."

"Yeah, great," Lewis said. "You happen to remember what they look like?"

"Are you kidding?"

"No," Lewis said testily. "I'm not kidding. I want information about a Mr. and Mrs. Henry Moore and I don't want smart-aleck answers. Now think. Are you positive you don't remember them at all?"

The receptionist's voice was more respectful as he said, "No, sir. I've been here fourteen years and I've seen almost a million customers come and go. I don't remember either names or faces."

"Is there anybody there who might?"

"Way back last February? Maybe a chambermaid, maybe a busboy or bellhop. I couldn't say but I doubt it."

Lewis asked the names of the chambermaid who handled the Moores' room and the bellhops who were on duty when they registered and checked out. While he waited for this information he thumbed gloomily through the pages of the passenger list. Nearly seven hundred people were aboard the *Alkmaar*.

It was fifteen minutes before the receptionist returned to the

line. He had the name of the chambermaid but she had left in
April and he didn't know her whereabouts. There had also been
a big turnover in bellhops and only one was still with them. "I
asked him," he said. "You can talk to him if you want but he
says he doesn't remember."

Lewis got the man's name and hung up. He lighted another
cigarette, mashing out the one that had died in the tray, and
looked at the list again. The Moores had cabin number 625 on
C deck. He turned to the "A's" on the list and started through
the alphabet noting the names and addresses of everyone else
on C deck.

It was a half hour job going through the nearly seven hundred
names and he had a list of sixteen families when he was through.
Two were in New York City, one lived in Bridgeport and the
others were scattered over the country at greater distances.

Lewis started with the New York families. The first call got no
answer and the second produced an operator who said the line
had been disconnected. He tried the Bridgeport family next and
got a Mrs. Tarrell on the phone. "Moore?" she asked. "Henry
Moore? Yes, I remember him. Very personable young man."

"Do you remember Mrs. Moore?" Lewis asked.

"A young dark-haired girl?"

For the first time in his days of drudgery Lewis felt his pulses
quicken. "Is that what she looked like? Dark-haired? Young?"

"Yes. A very lovely thing. I only saw her once or twice. She
was in her cabin most of the time. Her husband brought her up
for the dancing the second night out. I remember that. They
made a handsome couple."

"Tell me, Mrs. Tarrell. Was her first name Elizabeth?"

Mrs. Tarrell said, "Search me. I never heard her first name."

"Do you think you could identify her picture?"

She hesitated. "Yes. I think I could. I remember Mr. Moore
better, but I think I could."

"If I sent someone to your place in the next hour or two,
would you be home?"

"Yes, of course, if it would help."

Lewis hung up and found Lerner, Jim Daniels, and the New

York detective looking at him. "You got something?" Lerner asked.

"I may have. Woman in Bridgeport. I'm going to call the chief and see if he can send someone over to her with a picture."

CHAPTER XVIII

Chief Fellows got the call just before noon and what had become, for him and the Stockford force, a nearly dead case leaped to life again. "No kidding," he said. "And under the name 'Moore' too!" He took down Mrs. Tarrell's address, picked up the envelope of photographs and strode into the outer office where Wilks was writing up a stolen car report. "Want to take a ride to Bridgeport with me?"

Wilks, carefully pecking out his words, said, "Not especially. What for?"

"Just a possible break on the Betty Moore thing, that's all."

"Well, in that case!" Wilks closed the cover of the portable and got up. "What's the break?"

"A woman who knew a Mr. and Mrs. Henry Moore on board a ship."

Wilks grinned as he went for his topcoat. "Mrs. Henry Moore —and Mister? You mean the *lying* Mrs. Moore—the Mrs. Moore who doesn't have a husband and who uses a different name when she travels?"

"It sounds like that Mrs. Moore, yes, but you'd better not crow too soon. There're a lot of Mrs. Henry Moores in the world."

"But not very many," Wilks said, joining him at the door, "who'd make you drive to Bridgeport."

Mrs. Tarrell was a trim woman in her early forties with graying hair and a pretty face. She took in Fellows' gray shirt and gold badge when she answered his ring and said, "Oh, you must be from the police."

Fellows agreed with the surmise, made introductions and, with Wilks, followed the woman into a homey living room furnished in Colonial style. By the time she turned to indicate seats he had Betty's photographs out of their envelope and ready to hand her. "The first business is this, Mrs. Tarrell. Would you look at these and see if you recognize the girl?"

Mrs. Tarrell accepted the collection and pursed her lips for a moment over the top one. "Oh, but this is very good," she said, brightening. "It's an excellent picture. Yes, that's Mrs. Moore all right."

Fellows restrained himself from leaping with joy. "That's fine," he said. "That helps us a lot."

Mrs. Tarrell sorted briefly through the other pictures and nodded appreciatively at their quality. "These are all very good indeed. They're beautiful pictures." She handed them back and brought herself around to the business at hand. "Is there any particular reason why you're interested in the young woman? I thought it might be her husband you were after."

"You did?" Fellows arched an eyebrow.

"Or, perhaps, both of them. But you're only interested in her?"

"Not only, Mrs. Tarrell. But she does come first. Haven't you read about the girl who was killed on the beach at Indian Lake?"

Mrs. Tarrell pursed her lips again. "I might have," she said slowly. "I don't remember. Those things don't make much impression on me, I'm afraid. Do you mean to say Mrs. Moore is the woman who was killed?"

"She was, I'm sorry to say."

Mrs. Tarrell sank into a covered chair. "Oh, what a shame. The poor girl. Her poor husband."

"Yes," Fellows said, taking out his notebook and sitting down. "Her poor husband. You said, incidentally, you thought we'd be looking for him, or for both of them together. What does that mean?"

Mrs. Tarrell gestured deprecatingly. "It's probably nothing. Just a thought. I personally don't think he had anything to do with it. What made him—them—appear suspicious was the fact they left the ship in San Juan. People expected that of course they'd take the whole cruise and when there was the robbery and the Moores disappeared, why naturally people thought that they —well, he—was responsible."

Fellows eyed Wilks for a moment and slowly opened the note-book. "I see," he said. "This is something we didn't know about. We've been having trouble tracing her, finding out who she is."

"You mean Mr. Moore—uh—he isn't around?"

"Until now we haven't been sure there was a Mr. Moore. So I'd appreciate it very much if you'd tell us everything you can remember about them both, and about the robbery. In fact, everything about the cruise that might have anything to do with it or them."

She said, "Of course," and leaned forward a little. "Do you mean you think her husband killed her? I'm sure that's wrong. They were so obviously in love and she was such a beautiful, lovely girl."

"And what about him, Mrs. Tarrell? What was he like?"

She smiled. "A very handsome chap. Around middle twenties, I'd say, and most attentive. I really thought they were honey-mooners and I was so surprised to learn they'd been married over five years. She must have been just a baby and he not much more."

"But there was talk that he robbed some of the passengers?"

"There was talk but I don't put any stock in it. Nobody knew who did it and he was only suspected when he and his wife didn't return to the ship. The purser saw them go ashore with a couple of suitcases late in the afternoon and nobody saw them again after that. The robberies weren't discovered until that evening and, of course, the captain and the crew handled things until the next day when it was found that the Moores hadn't come back aboard. Then the police in San Juan were notified. Whether they found the Moores or not I don't know but they apparently hadn't by the time we sailed three days later."

Fellows brought the woman back to a chronological recital of the cruise and she smiled and said, "The *Alkmaar* sailed from Hoboken on February twelfth, that was a Tuesday, at noon. My husband and I had a cabin on C deck. I don't remember the number now, and we only just got under way, just about got past the Statue of Liberty when the dinner gong sounded. There was the usual to-do over signing up for tables. There were two servings and all the families with children ate at the first. My husband and I chose the second and we were assigned a table with two other couples. I don't recall their names but one was an elderly couple from Ohio and the other was a young couple from somewhere out west. She was German and they'd met when he was assigned over there in the service a few years back.

"I remember we were seated and the other people were still coming in and the girl said something to her husband in German, looking at someone just coming by. It was Mrs. Moore, as a matter of fact, and that was the first time I saw her. She and Mr. Moore were going to a table just back of us. The husband looked up at her and nodded at what his wife was saying."

"Did they know Mrs. Moore?"

"No, and she didn't notice them. They just looked at her as she passed. As a matter of fact, I asked if they knew her and the man laughed and said no, that his wife was asking what he thought of her looks. His wife spoke English fluently and I don't know why she made her remark in German unless it was a little more suggestive than merely how he'd rate Mrs. Moore as an appealing woman."

"And Mrs. Moore wasn't aware of this?"

"No. She was hunting her table number. I was facing their table, by the way, and I couldn't help noticing Mr. Moore. They were seated with two older couples and Mr. Moore seemed quite animated. He made friends with the others right away. Mrs. Moore was quiet and didn't have much to say but her husband more than made up for it. He had a very definite appeal. He was a very friendly, outgoing person, the kind everyone remembered,

very handsome and at ease and sort of uninhibited. His wife
was the kind of girl people—men, that is—would turn to stare at
but I think he made the more lasting impression.

"We saw them both in the lounge later in the afternoon with
some other people. He was laughing and talking and making
them laugh and the girl—his wife—she sat and watched him with
adoring eyes. I think that's when I came to believe they were
honeymooning."

Fellows said, "She was part of the background to him, would
you say?"

"Oh, no," Mrs. Tarrell hastily corrected. "He was the extro-
vert. He did most of the talking, but his remarks included her
and she laughed with the others at what he said."

"And you met them yourself?"

"Yes. At this point I didn't know who they were but they
caught your attention. Then when they had lifeboat drill—it was
late afternoon about four o'clock—the Moores and we had the
same station. Mrs. Moore was having trouble getting her jacket
on properly and he helped her and was very cute about it. My
husband and I were smiling at them and he said something to
us about his wife can get anything into a suitcase but she can't
get herself into a lifejacket. We got talking and they introduced
themselves and that's when I asked if they were honeymooning.
He burst out laughing and turned to her and said, 'How's that
for a compliment?' Then he told us they'd been married five and
a half years."

She paused and thought. "Now let me see, what happened
next? Oh yes. Dinner was at seven thirty and Mr. Moore came
alone. I could hear him tell the people at his table that his wife
wasn't feeling well. As a matter of fact, it was a little rocky that
day and a number of people didn't appear for dinner. I'm afraid I
couldn't resist saying to him when we were leaving that I hoped
she was all right. He said she was taking pills and would probably be right as rain the next day. Then we saw him in the evening in the lounge. They had dancing there and he showed up
alone again. He had a few drinks with a group he seemed to be
with but he also circulated among other groups. We hadn't been

out twelve hours and already he knew an amazing number of people.

"He did some dancing too and I must admit I was pleased to note that he didn't dance with any of the young single girls. Married five years and without his wife around you might have thought—. Anyway, he danced with the wives he'd met and, as a matter of fact, he danced once with me. He was a very good dancer, I might add."

"You talk to him much?" Fellows asked. "About himself, I mean."

"We talked but he didn't say much about himself. I do remember asking him what his work was, though. He was on vacation, he said, and he was—what was it? An engineer, I believe. He worked for Pratt-Whitney in Hartford. I think he said he was an aeronautical engineer. Anyway, I do remember he worked for Pratt-Whitney."

"Then he'd live in Hartford?"

"I presume so. I don't recall if he said."

Fellows made notes. "Anything else?"

Mrs. Tarrell reflected. "I didn't see Mrs. Moore the next day. She wasn't in for meals and he said she was still under the weather. I did see him here and there, though. He was very popular, particularly with the older couples. In fact, he seemed to gravitate to the older people—not elderly by any means, but older than himself.

"Then in the evening Mrs. Moore appeared and he squired her most attentively. He danced with a few other people and so did she but for the most part they danced with each other and in between times they were always holding hands."

Mrs. Moore, she went on, missed a couple of meals on Thursday as she recalled but was present for dinner. Mrs. Tarrell didn't see either of them thereafter until late in the evening when Mr. Moore came up to the lounge alone. The last she saw of him that night was after the midnight snack and just before she retired. Moore was drinking in the smoking lounge with another couple.

On Friday she thought Mr. Moore appeared alone for breakfast but wasn't sure. In any event, she didn't see either of them again. "We docked in San Juan, Puerto Rico, at noon and my husband and I went ashore. We didn't get back till dinner and I remember the Moores weren't there. I assumed they were eating ashore and I didn't think any more of it.

"Then, when we went to the lounge later in the evening we found everybody talking and there was a lot of upset. A number of cabins had been raided while the passengers were ashore in San Juan and quite a lot of money and valuables had been stolen. People, particularly those who'd been robbed, were blaming the stewards and the story was that the captain was questioning them.

"I didn't hear what the outcome of that was though I was told a thorough search of the stewards' quarters was made and the next day, I understand, the crew made a thorough search of the ship.

"The passengers still thought the stewards were responsible because the cabins were supposed to have been locked, but then the captain came into the dining room while we were eating. He ate in the other dining room himself, with the deluxe passengers. Anyway, he talked to the boy who waited on the Moores' table. The Moores weren't there and they hadn't been all day and we were all beginning to notice it.

"Later on I was told that the captain searched the Moores' cabin and looked very grim when he came out. Someone heard from the crew that their cabin was empty and their suitcases gone.

"There was a lot of ugly talk that night about the Moores. People were now blaming them for the thefts and it was said that the only people who had been robbed were people who'd been friendly with the Moores and who'd had them in their cabins for a drink or a little party. They were sure he'd managed some way to fix the locks so he could get back in.

"For myself, I don't know. They just didn't seem the type at all. Anyway, the rumors were that the San Juan police were hunting for them but we didn't hear any more and we didn't see the Moores again."

She was through with her tale and Fellows thanked her. "One thing. Would you describe Mr. Moore as accurately as you can?"

She said, "Yes. Let me see. I'd put him six feet in height, almost exactly six feet. I can tell because I danced with him. Black hair, dark brown eyes. Slender build but well developed. About a hundred and sixty pounds, I'd say. White skin. No noticeable marks or scars. Very good-looking, handsome in fact, but nothing distinctive about his face. It's hard to describe a face like his. Not an oval face or a round face but more long but not really long. Sort of lean without being thin."

"You'd know him if you saw him again?"

"Oh, yes. I'd know him more readily than I'd know his wife."

There were a few other questions and then the interview was over and the detectives went back to the car. "Maybe she didn't change her name," Fellows growled, starting the engine, "but I'm right when I called her a liar."

"Because of the robbery? That's only circumstantial evidence."

"Not the robbery. Her husband's death. If they're not a couple of crooks, then he *does* work at Pratt-Whitney and if he'd been killed in an accident, Motor Vehicles would have said so." He shifted gears and added, "But that's the first thing to check. I have a sneaking suspicion we aren't going to find him at Pratt-Whitney and, if not, then I'm going to look for him in the criminal files. Either he's a dead aeronautical engineer, killed in some unreported accident, or he's an out-and-out con man and that girl was his partner."

Wilks sat back. "Make your case," he said. "I still don't think she's the type."

CHAPTER XIX

Ed Lewis had found the right Betty Moore but his work was far from finished. Fellows called him up with congratulations as soon as he got back to the office and followed that with a new series of tasks. There was the registration card Henry Moore had filled out at the hotel in New York. "We want that," Fellows said, "or a photostat."

The robbery of the passengers opened new leads and Fellows went after them hard. There were the San Juan police to contact for whatever information they had. There were inquiries to be made of the shipping line for the names of the robbery victims. "See what you can learn from them," the chief said. "Find out if they had insurance and see what the insurance companies have to say. See if any of the missing jewelry has turned up. See what they know about this guy Moore."

Most important, of course, was how and when the Moores had returned to the States and Fellows wanted this problem tackled first. "Start with the airlines that service Puerto Rico," he said. "If those two were guilty they probably got the first available plane back. Check the airlines passenger lists and don't overlook the possibility of a false name. The ship docked at noon on the fifteenth of February so take it from there. One other thing. I want to know whether they booked passage on the *Alkmaar* for the whole cruise or just to San Juan."

When he was through with Lewis, Fellows called Lt. Biloxi of the State Police for a routine check for Henry Moore in the criminal files and for help in tracing his supposed employment at Pratt-Whitney. That done, he sat back and rubbed his hands together. "Well, Sid, things are beginning to percolate at last." He put on a triumphant grin. "You still think she's a saint? You think she's the widow of a Pratt-Whitney aeronautical engineer? Or do you think she and her husband—or pretended husband— were a confidence team working the ships? I wonder what she was *really* doing during those meals she missed."

"I notice," Wilks retorted, "that she didn't change her name when she came to Stockford, as per your theory. I also regard the beach at Indian Lake as a most extraordinary place for a confidence man, working the ships, to pick to strangle his partner. The partner, I might add, who helped him rob the passengers so successfully."

If Henry Moore was the con man Fellows suspected, the State Police had no record of it. Biloxi reported that fact to Fellows the same evening and it formed mild support for Wilks' belief that the girl was not an out-and-out liar, a point Wilks was quick to make the following day.

If she were not, however, it was soon learned that her husband was. Pratt-Whitney not only had no such man in their employ, they had never heard of him. This was not disappointing news to the Stockford chief for Fellows had wisely refrained from pinning any hopes on tracing Henry Moore through the aircraft plant. All the information did was confirm his conviction that handsome, charming, dashing Henry Moore was a thief and liar and, almost certainly, since the evening of August thirty-first, a murderer as well.

The call on which the chief did pin his hopes came in on Friday morning. Ed Lewis was on the line from New York and there was excitement in his voice. "Chief," he announced, "I think I've got something."

"Good," Fellows said with grim satisfaction and drew over his pad. "Shoot."

"In the first place, I've got the photostat of the hotel registration for you and I also found out the Moores booked passage for the whole cruise. About the passengers who were robbed, I don't have their names yet—"

"Never mind about them. What about the passenger lists for the planes?"

"Chief, San Juan did that for us. We got in touch with the San Juan police. They never did find the Moores but they checked the airports and found out a couple answering their description flew from San Juan to New York later in the day the ship docked. They booked themselves as Henry and Betty Cooper."

"Do they have anything more than just a description to say it's the same couple?"

"Yes, sir, they do. This Henry and Betty Cooper listed their address as Youngstown, Ohio, and put down as next of kin a Mr. and Mrs. C. W. Cooper, also of Youngstown. This was checked out and it's a phony. There aren't any such people in Youngstown."

Fellows nodded. "They're the ones then. Anything more on them?"

"Only that the plane landed in New York at two fifteen A.M. on the morning of February sixteenth. Where they went after that they don't have any idea."

"It's anybody's guess," Fellows admitted. "That's not so good."

"They might have put up at a hotel," Lewis said helpfully. "We could check all the Coopers who signed in on that date. It would have been around four in the morning."

"We could but I don't think it'd do us any good. Even if we did find them it's a cinch any forwarding address would be as phony as C. W. Cooper in Youngstown. And, like as not, they took the first train out of Grand Central. No, don't go after the hotels, at least not yet. Find out what you can about the passengers who were robbed and what information the insurance companies have."

"Sure thing, Chief. They might have a big file on Henry Moore."

"They might," Fellows agreed and hung up. "But," he muttered aloud to himself as he tore off the pages of notes from the pad, "I'll bet a dollar they don't have a damned thing."

He added the new information to the thin file on Elizabeth Moore and picked up one of her pictures. "You poor, poor fool," he said to it unhappily. "Why did you make it so easy for him and so hard for us?"

CHAPTER XX

Sid Wilks came into headquarters at noon with a paper bag in his hand. He shivered and said to Harris, subbing at the desk, "Lucky you. It's a raw wind out there." He opened the door to Fellows' office and found the chief poring over the Elizabeth Moore file at the table. "Well, it's finally happened," he said. "That desk of yours has got so cluttered it's driven you out. In another five years those papers will have you pinned in a corner." He set the bag beside the chief, took out a carton of coffee and put it in front of him. "A present. You look as if you could use it too."

"I've been thinking," the chief said.

"You don't look as if it agrees with you." Wilks opened his own container of coffee and sat in the chief's chair. "What's up?"

"The Moores came back to the States February sixteenth using the name of Cooper."

"Lewis found that out? Well, that's progress in the right direction."

Fellows shook his head. "But where do we go from there? Where did *they* go from there?"

"Yeah," Wilks said more soberly. "That's a very good question."

"I've been racking my brains. Jumping ship in San Juan after an out-and-out robbery doesn't sound like a couple of people who make a racket out of cruises. They couldn't work that kind of an operation very long. So I don't think we'd get anywhere trying to find Henry Moore or Henry Cooper on board ships. But from the way he played up to the older women on that cruise

I'd guess that's his technique; ingratiate himself, get in with some old dame, let her buy him gifts, maybe lift a few things here and there, maybe try a little blackmail. The trouble is, he can do that anywhere."

"And," put in Wilks, "he wouldn't need a partner. A wife would be more of a handicap than a blessing."

Fellows smiled faintly. "Still trying to whitewash her, Sid?"

"Just helping add up the score."

"Well, it doesn't add up to any number we can work with. From the sixteenth of February till the twenty-third of August that girl could have been anywhere, doing anything. Whatever led to her murder happened in there and we can't find it out unless we can find out about her."

Wilks made a face. "You've got no leads at all?"

"There're the insurance companies and, of course, the FBI. One of them might have a criminal file on Henry but it's a pretty slim chance."

"It all hangs on them, huh?"

"It looks like it, damn it. Lewis got a photostat of his hand-writing for us but unless there's something to match it with I don't know what good that'll do us."

"Handwriting? Handwriting!" Wilks sat up. "What was the name they used flying back? 'Cooper'? I'll tell you where I'd look for them first, Fred. In Pittsfield."

"Pittsfield? Why?"

"Handwriting reminded me. Didn't Betty Moore get a letter from Pittsfield on August thirtieth? If Henry wasn't killed in any auto accident he might be the one who wrote it. Even if it wasn't from him it would have been from someone they knew and that would put them in Pittsfield too."

Fellows looked up and his eyes widened slowly. "Damn it, Sid, if I don't think you might be a detective." He smote himself on the forehead. "Where are my brains? I'll bet that's it."

They went out to the main desk for the Pittsfield phone book and opened it on the big table. There were two possibilities, Henry A. Cooper at 1647 Ash Street and H. M. Cooper at 248

Sternwood, and they tried Henry A. first. That got them Mrs. Henry A., a widow with an ancient voice.

The second call produced another woman but she wasn't Mrs. Henry Cooper. Her husband's name was Horace.

"Damn," Fellows said, hanging up the phone. "I thought we had something."

"It was a long shot," Wilks told him.

"Yeah, but I like it. Pittsfield fits in here someplace."

"They might have used a new name, of course."

"Not Moore, though. Crouch has been through all the Moores." Fellows frowned and pulled at his chin. "If the girl did come from Pittsfield, she switched her name back to Moore from something else. If so, why wouldn't the something else be 'Cooper'? Why just use that name for the plane ride and discard it? People who use aliases usually stick with them to avoid confusion." He stopped suddenly and snatched up the phone book. "Say, what the hell am I thinking of? When did this book come out?"

"How would I know?"

"Before they moved there and got a phone, maybe?" He lifted the receiver and dialed information and said to Wilks, "I still bet it's Pittsfield."

The operator, however, was discouraging. She looked up Henry Cooper under new numbers but reported there weren't any.

Fellows kept plugging. "This man would have had a phone put in sometime after the sixteenth of February. Maybe it's been disconnected. Could you check and see if anybody named Henry Cooper has had phone service in Pittsfield at any time between February sixteenth and now? You might check the unlisted and private numbers too, if you would."

"If he has an unlisted number we can't give it to you," the girl said.

"I'm not worried about what the number is. I just want to know if he had a phone."

The operator said she'd have to call back and Fellows gave her the number. He retrieved his carton of coffee from the office and returned, opening it. Wilks said, "Of course there's always the city directory."

"Hah," Fellows answered. "Fat chance of his living there long enough to be in it." He paced the floor, sipping coffee as he did, stopped to study Betty's picture on the bulletin board and read the notices, resumed the pacing and came back almost leisurely to the phone when it rang.

"Chief Fellows?" the operator's cheerful voice said, "I looked it up and I'm sorry to say there's been no phone service of any kind for any Henry Cooper during the period you mention. If I can help you further, I'll be glad to."

"No," Fellows said. "That'll be all, I guess. Thank you." He hung up and downed the rest of his coffee in a gulp.

"No dice?" Wilks said. "Well I guess it wasn't a very good idea."

Fellows crumpled the container and gave it to Harris to drop in the basket behind the desk. "Would he necessarily have a phone?" Fellows asked, pulling again at his chin. "The way they travel and sever past connections everywhere they go, what would they want a phone for?"

"You're still bucking for Pittsfield?"

"Yes I am." The chief took out his chewing tobacco and gestured with the packet. "As you pointed out, that's where the letter came from and I don't know who else but Henry could have written it. So if he sent the letter from Pittsfield I'm going to look for him in Pittsfield." He turned. "Harris, get hold of Chief Crouch for me, will you? I'll take the call in the office."

Chief Crouch was as amiable as usual and Fellows told him he needed more help in the Elizabeth Moore case. "We think she and her husband lived in Pittsfield under the name of Cooper. This would be after the sixteenth of last February and they probably would have rented something. It could be a room in a boarding house, it could be an apartment, a house, a hotel, motel, trailer space in a park, even the YM and YWCAs."

"You want us to run a check on all those places?"

"That's what I want—anyplace where they could hang a hat, including spare rooms from the classified ads."

"It might take a few days."

"That's all right. We're used to waiting. Want me to assign you a couple of men?"

"Not yet. It might not be necessary unless we have to check the classifieds. I've got a couple of detectives doing nothing but organizing files. I can put them to work. Let me make sure I've got it straight, now. Henry Cooper's the name? Henry and Betty Cooper? Either one or both?"

"That's right."

"I'll let you know."

CHAPTER XXI

"Chief from headquarters. Chief from headquarters."

Fellows, cruising Stockford on a routine inspection at half past two that same afternoon, picked up his mike. "Fellows."

"Message from Pittsfield, Chief. Crouch just picked up a rent for Henry Cooper."

Fellows slowed behind a heavy truck. "Any details?" he said into the mike.

"He says the Ryder Real Estate Agency in Pittsfield rented a house to a Mr. and Mrs. Henry Cooper at 44 Glenwood Road on March first on a year's lease. He wants to know do you have any instructions? He's on the line right now."

Fellows depressed the mike button. "Tell him I'm coming up. Tell him I want to see the house. And get hold of Sid Wilks."

"Wilks is here."

"Sid," Fellows said into the mike, "get the girl's pictures and stand by. I'll pick you up."

Chief Crouch was in possession of a key to the house in ques-

tion when Fellows and Wilks walked into his office in the Pittsfield Police Department a half hour later. "I'm calling off the
search till we check this one out," he said, coming around his
desk to shake hands. "That all right with you?"

Fellows nodded. "The one you've got sounds hot."

"I've sent for my car. It'll be here in a minute." The buzzer
on his desk sounded and he talked into the phone for a minute
and hung up. "I'm no great shakes as a chief of police," he said,
"but I run a good department. Detective Kelly picked that one
up first off. I didn't think it'd be that easy."

"Neither did I," said Fellows. "You don't know how hard
he's been to trace."

"If we've traced him now," put in Wilks.

Crouch arched an eyebrow. "There's a question?"

"Don't mind him," Fellows said. "It was only his idea that
the guy came to Pittsfield."

"It was only an idea," Wilks said. "Now Fred thinks it's
gospel."

"It fits the requirements, such as the girl or this guy Cooper
knowing about Indian Lake."

The buzzer sounded a second time and Crouch took another
call. "This place is a beehive all the time," he complained when
he put the phone down again.

"You sending somebody with us to his house?"

"I'm going myself. It's an excuse to get out of here for a while.
Besides, I'd like to be in on the finish of this case of yours. Let's
hope there's an arrest to make."

"I'd like to be in on the finish of it too," Fellows said. "It's a
year's lease, you say? We might just be lucky enough to find the
guy home."

A plump, pink-faced, white-haired policeman with a mild manner and a bland face came in. "The car's out front, sir," he said,
fawning a little and stepping carefully out of everyone's way.

"That's what I want to hear, Mac," Crouch told him and
headed out the door.

The car was Crouch's official transportation, a black Cadillac
sedan with jump seats. Crouch, who was nearly as large as Fel-

lows and Wilks, didn't crowd into the back with them. He rode
with the driver, his body twisted so he could talk to his guests.
The talk was about the case with Fellows and Wilks filling him
in on details until the Cadillac slowed to a stop in front of a
modest-sized bungalow with a small, untended patch of lawn in
front. A wooded lot was on the right and a similar but better-
kept house on the left.

The window shades of the bungalow were drawn and Crouch,
shifting his bulk to peer through his side windows, said, "Don't
look like anybody's home."

"And for quite a while," Fellows added dourly. "That's not
too good."

The three policemen got out and went up the walk to the
front door leaving the driver in the car. Fellows pressed the bell
and they could hear the sound of it from deep inside but the
ring had an emptiness to it that went with the house. Fellows
rattled the locked front door, rang again, but didn't wait. He
started around the side that faced the woods, walking slowly,
eyeing all that came in sight, while Wilks and Crouch followed.
At the back door he tried the knob but it didn't turn either.
"Locked tight," he said.

"Want to go in and look around?" Crouch said, producing
the key.

"Let's try next door first. Where're the girl's pictures, Sid?"

"I left them on the back seat."

"Bring them along if you will and we'll see what we get."

The three walked out to the front again by the driveway between the two houses and Fellows rang the bell of 42 Glenwood
Road. In a moment the curtains at the front window parted
and dropped back, then the door was opened by an attractive
brunette woman in her early thirties holding a baby. She looked
at the uniforms on the two big men, at the official looking
Cadillac by the curb and at Wilks, in a brown suit, crossing her
lawn with a large manila envelope in his hand. The baby looked
too and started to cry.

"We're police officers," Fellows said by way of introduction, "and we're interested in the family who lives next door. They don't seem to be home."

The woman held the baby against her shoulder and patted his back. "There, there," she said. "Nice men, Danny. Nice men. They won't hurt you." To Fellows she said, "No, they've gone away."

"Cooper is their name. Is that right?"

"Yes. Will you come in?" She stepped back and said, "There, there, Danny. Don't cry, baby."

The three large men stepped into the living room and seemed to fill it. Fellows made more formal introductions and learned the woman's name was Mrs. Mabel Sears. She sat down on a chair and cuddled the wailing baby on her lap. "He's not used to strangers," she said apologetically. "I think perhaps the uniforms frighten him."

Fellows said the police were great at frightening children and showed her one of the portrait photos. "Could you tell us, is this Mrs. Cooper?"

"Yes, that's Mrs. Cooper." She rocked the baby and said, "Shush, Danny, Mommy's looking at a picture." She frowned slightly. "There's something about that picture that seems familiar but I can't imagine where I could have seen it. She didn't have any around that I remember."

"In the newspapers perhaps?"

"Yes. That might be it." She looked up. "Was it in the papers?"

"It's been in the papers a number of times, Mrs. Sears. This is the girl who was strangled on Indian Lake beach Labor Day weekend."

Mrs. Sears started. "Mrs. Cooper? You mean she's the one who was strangled? I thought it was—" She sank back in numbed dismay and the baby howled louder. "Oh, good heavens."

"We're trying to locate her husband, Mrs. Sears," Fellows said, raising his voice above the baby's and glancing at the creature with distraction. "We'd like to ask you a few questions."

"Yes," she said, still shocked. She rocked the baby absently for a moment, then grew aware of his shrill cries. "Wait," she said,

rising. "Let me put him in his playpen." Fellows nodded his relief and she went off muttering, "Mrs. Cooper? Oh, the poor
woman."

The baby howled louder when he was put down but at least
he was farther away. Mrs. Sears closed a door which dimmed
the sounds still further and returned, pale of face and brushing
back a lock of hair. "I had no idea," she said. "Whatever could
have happened?"

"That," Fellows told her, "is what we're trying to find out.
What we'd like from you is everything you know about Mrs.
Cooper and about her husband."

"I'm afraid I don't know much," she said, smiling wanly and
sitting down again. "They moved in on the first of March. I do
remember that."

"Did you get to know them at all?"

"Somewhat. I called on Mrs. Cooper the first week to be
neighborly and found her to be a very sweet girl. We were friendly
after that. Not close, but friendly. We'd have a cup of coffee together now and then, especially after her husband left. She
adored him and was very lonely after he got transferred."

"Transferred?"

"Yes. He worked for the Army as a civilian and they sent him
overseas in July. Betty, Mrs. Cooper, was very disappointed.
She was so set up about the house. She told me it was the first
time in their married life they'd been able to settle down. Married six years, she said, and constantly on the go. She was so
young. It was hard to believe she'd been married so long. And,
poor thing, she so longed to have a home of her own and a family. It was almost touching to see her with Danny. She loved
babies and wanted more than anything to have one herself."

Fellows said, "Did she tell you what they were doing when
they were always on the go, where they went?"

"No. I only know it was her husband's business. They were
constantly moving, living out of a suitcase to hear her tell it. An
apartment here, a boarding house there, a furnished room someplace else. That's why she was so set up about having a house.
That girl was a homebody if there ever was one. I mean these

houses here aren't much and we're only in this one till we can manage something better, but to her it was like living in a palace." She cocked her ear to the baby's screaming and looked tempted to retrieve him. She forced herself to laugh. "I mean she envied me. Can you imagine that? Just because I have a husband whose job keeps him in one place and I have a baby. It's nice and all but Danny, well, he hates to be left alone. The minute I put him down he cries. I really don't know why it should be so important to her."

She was looking a little distraught about the baby and Fellows pulled her back to the subject. "You said her husband got transferred?"

Mrs. Sears looked up at him again. "Yes. It was all right for him, I suppose, but I really felt sorry for her. She'd been living in such a glow. She really thought it was going to work out this time, I mean the settling down and raising a family. She said pretty soon they'd have enough money saved so he could get into a different line of work where he wouldn't have to move all the time." She looked pained once more at the baby's shrieks. "Maybe if I got him a bottle?"

"It does him good to cry," Fellows said.

"Good? What about his psyche?"

"I have four children and it didn't hurt theirs any."

"You mean you *let* your children cry?"

"When they were naughty I also *made* them cry. Now if we could get back—"

Mrs. Sears came to her feet. "My Danny happens to be a very sensitive child. This could do him terrible harm. Excuse me."

She disappeared in the direction of the howls and Fellows, who had stood up with her, sighed. Wilks said, "You'd better not antagonize the lady with your theories on child-raising. We need her more than she needs us."

Fellows said, "Well I don't need Danny. How do we talk to her with a bawling child around?"

"Wait for his nap."

"Yeah. Law and order waits for nap time."

The sounds of sobs lessened and were replaced by the woman's cooing noises. Mrs. Sears reappeared cradling a teary baby and said, "See, he's quiet now. He just didn't like being alone."

The baby looked at the three men and started to wail again. Mrs. Sears forced an unhappy smile. "He's not used to men," she explained. "You should have seen him coo when Mrs. Cooper came in. He adored her." She resumed her seat and said to the child, "There, there. Mommy won't let the naughty old men hurt her Danny."

Fellows sat down facing her again and took a gold watch with a leather fob from his watch pocket and dangled it. It glinted and rotated slowly and the baby stopped crying to stare. "So for a few months," he said to Mrs. Sears, "Henry Cooper worked in Pittsfield?"

"Mr. Cooper?" She watched the baby's interest in the swaying object while she brought herself back to her erstwhile neighbors. "They lived here but I don't know where he worked or what he did. He was away most of the time. It was her only fly in the ointment, I guess. He'd be gone for days on end and then he'd come around for a night or two and then he'd be off again. She never complained but it was hard for her. She wasn't the complaining type, I guess. I'd've had the screaming meemies." She smiled at the baby. "No, Danny. You can't have the watch. Just look at it."

Danny was reaching and his face started to pucker. Fellows surrendered and gave him the watch. "He can't hurt it," he said over Mrs. Sears' concern. "What did Mrs. Cooper do all the time her husband was away?"

"Nothing," Mrs. Sears said, her attention on the child. "She kept the house. She was in love with keeping house. All the chores, the cleaning, the fixing, the upkeep, she loved them. I don't know how she kept herself busy with them but she did."

"She never went out?"

"Only to the stores a couple of blocks away. I tried to get her to go to the movies with us a couple of times and she did go with us once but you could tell it wasn't any fun for her without her husband."

Fellows said slowly, "All this moving around he did. That doesn't sound like the Army."

Mrs. Sears said, "Don't put it in your mouth, Danny, it's dirty. Now I don't know about that. I can't say for a fact he was working for the Army at that time. I do know that it was the Army that sent him overseas last July but maybe he changed jobs. She didn't talk about his work much. She didn't seem to know much about it, or care. Except that she didn't like moving all the time . . . Danny, stop. You'll get a disease . . . You know, I tried to persuade her once to put pressure on her husband to get some other kind of job. Believe me, I'd lay down the law to my Frank if he had a job like Mr. Cooper's. But she practically turned pale at the idea. I swear she doesn't know about female emancipation. What he said went. Where he went, she followed."

Wilks said, "I guess that shows Betty up as a con artist, all right, Fred."

Fellows ignored him. "What can you tell us about the husband? Did you know him?"

"I saw him. I knew him to say hello to, that was all. Young, dark-haired, good-looking man, very good-natured. Very pleasant."

"Personable, in other words?"

"Very personable. A little young to me but I can see why she idolized him. She seemed a little childish that way."

Danny dropped the watch on the floor and Mrs. Sears retrieved it and gave it back to him. "You must be careful of the man's watch," she said. "Remember, it's not yours."

Fellows eyed the child uneasily as Danny shook the watch by the fob and threw it down on the rug again. This time he picked it up himself. Mrs. Sears said, "Danny, that wasn't nice."

Fellows held the watch to his ear and then tucked it away. "What about Mrs. Cooper's leaving the house?" he asked. "You know anything about that?"

"She went overseas to join her husband. He sent for her. That's what I don't understand. I don't see how she could have come to be at Indian Lake. That's a mystery to me. She was supposed to be overseas. Apparently, for some reason, she didn't go."

Danny, deprived of the watch, crinkled his face and burst into tears once more. Wilks tried to hand him his key-chain but the baby pushed it away with louder howls. Fellows said, "She told you this?"

"It was this way," Mrs. Sears said, trying to rock the baby. "It was last month some time—I believe it was a Friday—when I happened to look out and notice a moving van next door. Mrs. Cooper hadn't said anything about moving and I was surprised. It was only a small van because they'd rented the house furnished and the only things being taken out were a few suitcases and a television and things like that. The van went away and I happened to be outside when Mrs. Cooper came out with a small suitcase. She said she was putting her things in storage, that her husband's job overseas was going to take longer than they'd thought and she was flying to join him. She didn't tell me where it was she was going but I got the idea it was Europe. I asked if they'd be moving back into the house and she said she didn't know, it depended on her husband's work. She hugged and kissed Danny and said goodbye and she walked to the bus stop up on Union Avenue and that was the last I saw of her."

"How did she act? Was she glad or sad?"

Mrs. Sears hugged the baby and cooed to him. "Naughty man take his watch away? That's all right, baby. We'll get you something else just as good. I can't say about emotion. I remember feeling sorry for her because she wasn't going to have that house and family she wanted after all, but she didn't seem unhappy herself. After all, she was going back to him and, house or no house, she'd been obviously lonely all by herself all summer and rather depressed. She wanted to talk to me more, be with me and the baby more, because she didn't have any friends or anybody else. I suppose when you're moving all the time you don't have much chance to make friends."

"Apparently not," Fellows agreed. "We've certainly had trouble finding people who knew her."

"She was a warm person, but shy. Her husband, I'm sure, had no trouble meeting people but I could see she would. Does her husband know she's dead? He must wonder why she never came overseas."

"This we don't know. You mention that she put her things in storage. You happen to notice the name of the company?"

Mrs. Sears didn't but she thought it began with a "V". She rocked the crying child and looked fretful. "Is there much more? I don't like Danny to be so upset."

"Only a couple of things. You say Mr. Cooper would come and go from the house. Did he have a car?"

"Yes. They bought a Volkswagen shortly after they moved in."

Fellows made a note of that. "One last thing. Did anybody ever come to visit them?"

She shook her head. "No, not once. They really flocked by themselves. She didn't seem to know a soul. Her husband probably had friends but he never brought them around."

Fellows thanked her and got up. He hesitated about patting the child on the head and thought better of it. If he touched him the baby might never stop crying.

The three went outside, leaving Mrs. Sears in her chair with Danny and the sounds of crying stopped. "Your watch still running?" Wilks asked.

"Yeah," Fellows said. "It's a good watch." He shook himself as if to shake the baby into the past and said, "Now let's try the *quiet* house and see what Mrs. Cooper left."

CHAPTER XXII

Crouch's key opened the front door and the three found themselves in a neat, tidy dwelling with a floorplan identical to the one they had left. It was immediately apparent, however, that it would be fruitless to wait there for the return of Henry Cooper. The undisturbed layer of dust that covered everything indicated he had long since abandoned the place.

Crouch said he'd have his fingerprint men go over the house but, as they wandered from room to room it became evident that few prints would be found. Underneath the layer of dust everything was spotless. In the bathroom the medicine cabinet was empty and the enamel polished. In the kitchen a carefully opened drawer revealed the cutlery placed just so.

"Loving care," Wilks said. "I guess she hated to say goodbye to her first home."

"What else did she have to do," Fellows retorted, "except keep the place clean?"

The search didn't take long for there weren't many places to look, nor was there anything to find. All that remained of Betty Cooper's six-month residency were the impersonal furnishings she had found when she came. Not so much as a stray piece of paper remained to throw light on the personality of the recent inhabitant. Betty had left the place in perfect order for the next tenant and, in so doing, had destroyed all traces of herself. "Too thorough," Fellows grumbled. "Hell, we'll be lucky if we can find one print the way she's cleaned everything. Maybe that was the idea. Maybe," he said, twitting Wilks, "that was her customary procedure."

They relocked the house and were about to leave when Fellows, on a sudden thought, opened the lid of the small metal mailbox nailed above the bell. "I ought to have my head examined," he said in annoyance. "Look what I almost missed." He lifted out a glassine windowed envelope which had "Van Meter Co., Moving and Storage. 16 Hartford St., Pittsfield, Conn." printed in the upper lefthand corner. "I guess this saves us having to track down the moving company." He opened the letter and pulled out a bill for $2.50 to cover storage through October. It was addressed to Mrs. Henry Cooper and the postmark dated the mailing as September eighteenth.

"I guess she figured Henry would have the stuff out of storage before the first of October," he said, tucking the envelope into his pocket. "I think we're in luck."

"Maybe he's cleaned it out of storage already," Wilks reminded him. "We haven't turned up any storage receipt so she must have had it in her purse and that means he's got it."

"What a cheerful guy you are."

They returned to the car and started back and Fellows said, "At least we're getting on the right track at last. You know, Crouch, that house there and that woman next door have given us the first concrete information we've gotten about that phantom Henry character. Every time the girl herself, who Sid thinks was so straight and honest, opened her mouth she told a different story. Every document Henry ever signed gave false information—everything from next-of-kin to last address. But now we've got him pegged with an automobile and that car is fact, not fiction. And we've got a moving company which might still have their personal possessions waiting for us. And we've got a rented house which means they must have got somebody to give them a reference. At last, thank God, we've got something we can get our teeth into."

Wilks said to Crouch, "This evil girl he's talking about, who never played around, never looked at another man, but spent all her time minding the home, might have made a couple of misstatements of fact—"

"A couple of misstatements of fact?" Fellows bellowed. "Why that girl never put two honest words close enough together to touch each other. She calls herself Mrs. Moore, then Mrs. Cooper, then Mrs. Moore again. God knows what she would have called herself next or what she called herself before."

"As I was saying," Wilks went on loftily, "this black sinner Fred tries to tar might have made a couple of misstatements of fact *on* her husband's orders, out of *loyalty*. Dumb loyalty perhaps, blind loyalty perhaps, but loyalty. This is a little different from the girl Fred sees who's going around making wax impressions of cabin locks on board ship while the other passengers are eating their meals."

"Look," Fellows said, "I've already said I don't think they worked the ships. So let her be sick in her cabin—with a bottle of dramamine to prove it. The fact remains that her husband is an obvious crook and she can't have been married to him for six years without finding it out no matter how deaf, dumb, blind and loyal she was."

"Six years?" Wilks smiled. "She must be getting through to you. It's only her sayso that she was married that long. Don't tell me you believe her?"

"I'll tell you I'll believe the Motor Vehicle Department and the moving company and the renting agent a damned sight faster."

Wilks shrugged. "Even I'll do that. You going to try to get to all of them today?"

"We can if we split it up. You take Motor Vehicles. I'll take the renting agent, and if you can spare somebody, Crouch, I'd like one of your men to try the moving company and see if her things are still there. We'd need a court order, I expect, to go through them if they are. Maybe you can arrange that."

"I can," Crouch said. "I don't know how soon I can get it."

The Cadillac let Fellows off at the Ryder Real Estate Agency and the others went on to their assigned tasks. It was an office in the downtown section of Pittsfield, second floor front of a building facing the green and half a block from police headquarters.

The chief waited for a rickety elevator and walked into a small front office that was tended by a receptionist. Mr. Ryder, she told him, was out but was expected back in half an hour. Fellows decided he'd wait and thumbed through a magazine. The wait, however, coupled with the food pictures in the magazine ads made him too hungry and he finished out the period in a nearby drugstore over a cup of coffee.

Ryder was in his office when the chief returned. He was a paunchy man with a bald head, shrewd eyes and a big cigar and he welcomed the policeman a little querulously. "What gives with this Cooper couple at 44 Glenwood Road?" he asked, shaking hands. "What's with them?"

"That's what we're trying to find out. What do you know about them?"

"Their name's Mr. and Mrs. Henry Cooper. Appeared to be a nice young couple. Took the place for a year. Want to see the lease?"

"I'd like to see the signature on the lease."

Ryder went to his file drawers, sorted briefly and produced it. He gave it to Fellows and stepped back, compressing his lips nervously. "Something wrong with the Coopers?"

"The house has been empty for more than a month, Mr. Ryder. You know that?"

"Empty? More than a month? No I didn't know. Vacation maybe?"

"No, I don't think it's any vacation." Fellows handed back the lease. "Do you have a duplicating machine? Could I get a copy of this signature somehow?"

"Ethel will do it." He took the paper out of the office to her and returned. "It's not a vacation, it's moving away? Why? Is it something you can tell me?"

"I can tell you. The girl's been murdered. We're trying to find her husband. Are they behind in the rent?"

"No. He paid the whole year in advance. Wouldn't seem to me he was expecting to move if he did that. So she got murdered and you think he did it, huh?"

"I don't know who did it but naturally we want to talk to the husband. Did he give you any references?"

"Sure thing." Ryder went into the file again and produced a letter. It was short and handwritten on pale gray unmarked stationery of good quality. The return address was "Pagel Real Estate, Tarrytown, New York" and the letter read:

"To Whom It May Concern:

"I have known Mr. and Mrs. Henry Cooper for the past four years as tenants and as friends. They are a quiet, serious, industrious young couple and two of the finest tenants I have ever had. They have my heartiest recommendation and I would be glad to vouch for them personally at any time.

"Respectfully yours,
"Courtney Pagel."

"It's a pretty good recommendation," Fellows said. "Did you ever confirm it?"

Ryder said, "Well, no, I never did. They'd paid in advance and I could size them up as a pretty stable couple. They didn't seem pressed for money and, well, I just never did."

Ethel came in with a copyprint of the last page of the lease containing Henry Cooper's signature and Fellows promptly compared it with the handwriting of the letter.

Ryder was too short to look over the chief's shoulder so he looked over his arm. "You think he wrote that letter himself?"

"I'm not that much of an expert but the writing does look similar. I don't like to bother you but could I have a photostat of the letter?"

"You can keep the letter itself if you want. Let it not be said that Charlie Ryder ever stood in the way of the police."

Fellows slipped the letter into his notebook as one more piece of the concrete evidence that was starting to come his way at last. He folded the copyprint and put that into his hip pocket, thanked the man and headed back to police headquarters and Crouch's large, neat, comfortable office.

Crouch was behind his desk on the telephone again and he waved the chief to a seat while he finished his call. "Wilks ain't back yet," he said, hanging up, "but I got good news for you. The Van Meter Company still has the girl's things. They'll let us go through the stuff if we can bring the proper legal papers but it's nearly five and I won't be able to get them till Monday

morning. Meanwhile, though, we've made it clear that if anybody comes to take those things out of storage, they're to notify
us and hold the guy till we get there."

"Has that October bill been paid?"

"Nope. Only through the end of this month. Only through
Monday."

"We'll come up Monday noon. Will you have the papers ready
by then?"

"Should have. Meanwhile, tomorrow we'll get the house fin-
gerprinted. You want copies sent to Hartford?"

"Yes, and Washington."

Wilks came in at quarter past five. He was chewing tobacco
and walked with a jaunty step. "We're getting closer," he said.
"Henry Cooper bought a tan Volkswagen secondhand from a
John Rhodes of 125 Service Street. Sale was recorded on Friday
March fifteenth."

"You got a license number for that car?" Fellows asked.

"That I have. Connecticut plates. Number is AM99874."

Crouch said, "I'll get that number right out. State Police, the
works. Tan, huh?"

"Unless it's been repainted," Wilks said.

Fellows got up. "We'll get going, Crouch. Expect us about one
o'clock Monday to go through the girl's things. If the papers
aren't going to be ready, you'd better call me."

"Sure thing."

The chief and Wilks walked out, down the corridor and onto
the outside steps, Fellows relating his experience with Ryder.

"Looks like we're closing in," Wilks said. "Another few days
ought to land the husband in our laps."

Fellows smiled. "So you think he's alive, eh? That's not the
way Betty told it, you know."

"He made her tell that widow story."

"How? By twisting her arm?"

"Nuts to you," Wilks said. "I still wouldn't mind having a
girl like her for a daughter."

CHAPTER XXIII

The weekend produced only two new pieces of information. The FBI had no record of Mr. Henry Moore-Cooper and Tarrytown had nobody in the area named Courtney Pagel. The latter news was fully expected for the photostat of Henry Cooper's hotel registration was in Fellows' hands now and the writing matched that of the faked letter of reference as well as the signature on the lease.

"We're getting there," Fellows told Wilks gleefully. "Now we can be sure we've picked up his handwriting."

Wilks was less enthused. "I'd rather pick up his car," he said.

The alarm for the car, however, had brought in nothing and the Volkswagen was still being sought Monday noon when the two made their trip back to Pittsfield to see what Betty had put into storage.

Crouch was waiting for them with the warrant when they arrived. "Came in at eleven," he said. "All neat and tidy. I even called the guy and said you'd be over. He's ready for you."

Fellows thanked him and scanned the paper, then tucked it in his pocket.

"There's bad news too," Crouch went on. "That girl really cleaned up that house. Two of my men went over it front to back and I mean they went over it. You know what? They didn't get one single perfect print. The best they could do was three partials."

The partials, Crouch went on to explain, had been sent to the Criminal Identification Bureau in Hartford. Two belonged to Betty and the third wasn't on file. Fellows shrugged that off as expected and left the office. What interested him at the moment was Betty Cooper's belongings.

The Van Meter Company was two blocks down the side street and a block and a half up Hartford. Fellows and Wilks didn't bother with a car in downtown traffic and walked the distance under chill skies and the threat of rain.

The building was a three story loft with show-windows in front displaying all manner of old stoves, refrigerators and other household objects which had been bought up or taken over for nonpayment of storage charges. The interior of the downstairs was a vast room with supporting columns and more rows of stoves, beds, couches and heavy pieces, arranged without regard to display advantages but only to allow aisles between. The ceiling was high, the lights dim and, in the dull cloudy light of the day, the effect was depressing.

Fellows and Wilks found the owner in a dingy cluttered office at the rear. He was a fat man with a stomach that thrust itself two feet in front of him so that he had to settle well back on his hips to keep from pitching forward. His beefy face was marked by thick lips, puffy circled eyes and a broad flat nose that looked like a glob of putty.

He waddled out, took the paper Fellows handed him and looked at it briefly. "Yeah," he said in a guttural voice and ran a hand like a ham over thinning gray hair. "Hey, Mike." He raised a shirt-sleeved arm the size of a large man's calf and gestured imperiously.

Mike, a lean black-haired lad wearing a pair of too large overalls and otherwise bare from the waist up, left off shifting a stove on a dolly and came over. "Show these guys the Cooper stuff. Third floor where I told you."

The youth said, "Yessir, Mr. Gorman," and led the way to a freight elevator beside the office. The barnlike car ground its way up two stops on an automatic button and the youth pushed down the bottom half of the split doors with his foot. The top half went up simultaneously and the trio stepped onto a concrete floor crammed with mountains of stored furnishings stacked to the ceiling with paths between.

Mike led the way through the labyrinth of aisles and stopped near the front windows to stare up at the top of a pile. "This is it," he said. He wheeled a handcart over and stood on it, decided he wasn't high enough and pulled a loose chair free from the pile and stood on that too. "Want to hold that truck steady?" he said as he tugged at the items jammed at the top.

He handed down a suitcase similar to the one the dead girl had had at Mrs. Fremont's, only larger. He passed down a second, then looked around and pulled a paper from his hip pocket. "Let's see. There's a bag of curtain material, a box of kitchen utensils, a box of bedding, two clothesbags and a television set. You want those things?"

Fellows said, "You can hold off on those till we see what's in the suitcases."

The boy climbed down agilely from the chair, pushed it back with its fellows on top of the adjacent stack and jumped lightly from the handcart. "Anything else?"

"These two suitcases the only suitcases?" Fellows asked as Wilks opened the first on the flat bed of the wheeled cart.

The boy consulted his list again. "That's all. Here, you want to see the manifest?"

Fellows waved it away. "That's all right. Thanks."

"You think she's got stolen goods in there?"

"We're just poking around," Fellows told him. "Thanks a lot."

The boy tarried for a moment before deciding he wasn't wanted. He turned and headed back up a long aisle to the rear and the elevator. Wilks was poking through clothes and there were a lot of them for the suitcase was tightly and expertly packed. "I don't know how she gets so much into these things," he said. "I'm scared to disarrange them. I'll never fit them back."

"Good quality clothes," Fellows said, glancing at the array. He laid the second heavy suitcase down, unfastened a restraining strap and popped the catches. "Thank God she didn't have these locked and the keys in that purse we never found. We'd need a crowbar the way they're made."

Wilks didn't answer. He'd found a snapshot folder tucked down in a corner and was pulling out half a dozen prints. "Here she is in a bathing suit," he said, handing the top one to the chief. "She really looks good in one."

Fellows glanced at it and laid it aside. "They all of her?"

"These are. Hold it. Here's a man. It must be Henry."

Fellows looked over Wilks' shoulder. "Take it to the light."

The two went over by the large, steel-framed frosted windows for a close look. The youth was in a bathing suit too, with the water at his back and the picture had been taken in bright sunlight so that the shadows were sharp and black. It was a full length picture of a lean man in lowcut trunks with his hands on his hips. He had black hair but the shadows cast by his eyebrows and nose made it difficult to tell what he looked like other than that he appeared to be nice looking. "Well, it gives us an idea at least," Wilks said.

"It matches the description we keep getting of him but it doesn't go much further. And that water doesn't tell us anything. No ships, no islands, nothing but horizon. It could be the Sound, the ocean, anything."

"Anything but Indian Lake." Wilks turned the picture over but the back was blank. He went through the rest of the lot but they were all of Betty in her bathing suit, obviously taken on the same beach the same day.

They returned to the suitcases again and it was Fellows who made the next discovery. He pulled out a packet of four letters wrapped with elastic, all in identical pale gray envelopes. The top one was addressed to Mrs. Henry Cooper at 44 Glenwood Road, Pittsfield and bore a Pittsfield postmark and the date, August 20. The handwriting and the paper were the same as the one Fellows had got from Ryder.

Wilks' eyes widened at the chief's find but Fellows, pulling the top letter from under the elastic, said, "You keep looking, Sid. I'll read you the dirty parts." He opened the letter, took it to the light and read aloud:

" 'Dear Betty,

" 'Maybe at long last things will work out. I know you've wanted a baby and I've been trying to arrange things. Forget the other things we've talked about. This is the important thing and now we can start to plan for it. I've wanted one too, God knows.

"'Here's what I want you to do. Put everything you have in storage and close up the house. I can't come to you there and we must meet at another place. I've explored all around and have found a good one. We won't be known there so it'll be O.K. and won't hurt the deal. Here's what you do.

"'As soon as you can get away, take the bus to Stockford. That's a town about twelve miles south of here. When you get to Stockford, take a Lake Ave. bus south. You get it on the northwest corner of Center and Meadow. Tell the driver you want to get off at a place called Little Bohemia. It's about two miles out. The driver will let you off at a road that goes to Indian Lake. It's the only public road. Walk up past the pavilion on your right and turn on Number Three Street. The third house in is Mrs. Fremont's. She has a number of rooms vacant and you'll have no trouble renting one if you get there before Saturday. Wait there till I get in touch with you.

"'Only take as few things as you absolutely must. You won't be there long and one small suitcase should do. If the Sears or anybody want to know why you're leaving Pittsfield, tell them you're joining me overseas. I presume that's where you've told them I am. Do it right, my girl, because I wouldn't want our plans to settle down and raise a family to go astray.

"'For the people in Little Bohemia, if they get nosey, you'd better have a different story. You are to register as Mrs. Elizabeth Moore because that's how I'm going to address you when I write again. Tell people you're a widow, that your husband was killed in an automobile accident three months ago. I'm spelling it out so you'll have it straight and won't slip up. You can explain why you've come there by saying your family is dead and you'd been staying with your in-laws, Mr. and Mrs. Henry Moore Senior. Don't say where they live if you can help it because somebody might get suspicious and check up. You never can tell. If you have to tell somebody, make it someplace in New York State. Tarrytown will do.

"'If they want to know why you left your in-laws, tell them you wanted to get away from it all. You can make it stronger by suggesting that a friend of your late husband's, make it the best man at your wedding, your husband's best friend, is making a play for you. And whatever you do, don't forget you're Mrs. Henry Moore again.

"'Be patient, Sweets, and do as I say and things will be beautiful. I'll be in touch as soon as I can.

"'Love,
"'H.

"'P.S. Destroy this letter. H.'"

Fellows looked up. "What do you think of that?"

Wilks, who had stopped going through the girl's suitcase to listen, said, "There's a nice snow job. He cons her with all that secret-deal-that-will-put-us-on-easy-street stuff in order to lure her to a spot for a murder. And she's a girl who did what she was told. All he had to do was say, 'We'll have a baby and settle down.'"

"Except, thank God, she didn't obey him and destroy the letter."

"It was all she had of him, I guess."

Fellows frowned. "So he scouts around and decides Little Bohemia is the place to do away with her. Why the hell would he pick that spot?"

"I suppose because it cuts her off from him. She goes around with a phony name and phony story and nobody can trace her. The husband, who should be the first suspect, becomes the last."

"But it takes a bold man to strangle a girl on a public beach with other people around."

"Boldness is one of his traits."

"I suppose." Fellows rubbed his chin. "I wonder if he used the 'settle down and have a baby' line with her down on the beach. That might have made her hold still for him while he slipped that cord around her neck."

"And robbed her body afterwards," Wilks said grimly. "Guys like him are the best argument I can think of for capital punishment. What about the rest of the letters? They show a motive?"

Fellows picked up the other three and returned to the window. "The first is postmarked July twenty-fifth. Mailed in Pittsfield again. They're all in Pittsfield."

"He didn't go very far away for that so-called Army job of his. I wonder why he didn't live with her."

"This may be an answer," Fellows said, scanning the letter. "'Dear Betty. Forget about the divorce talk. I didn't mean it. Enclosed is some money to take care of things. I've got a deal going and I'll be tied up for a while. I'll let you know as soon as I've got something definite. In the meantime, say nothing to anybody. Don't write anybody or call anybody. If the neighbors get nosey, tell them what I told you. I'm off on a job with the Army and you don't know when I'll be back. Love, H. P.S. Destroy this letter.'" Fellows folded the gray piece of stationery without comment and tucked it back in the envelope.

Wilks said, "So. He wanted out and she wouldn't let him go."

"Which means there's another woman," Fellows said, opening the next letter. "This one's dated July twenty-eighth. Let's see. 'Dear Betty. Just a line to let you know things are coming along fine. You'll never guess who I ran into in a swank New York restaurant Saturday. Peggy, of all people. Small world. She was with a girlfriend and they were in to go to a show. I was down there with this woman I'm cooking up the deal with which is going to set us up on Easy Street and make everything right with us for ever and ever.

"'Peggy said the family's fine. Ernie has a summer job driving a delivery truck. Peggy says Mrs. K fell off the stoop last month and hurt her back and uses a cane. She got two black eyes too. I'll bet she looked funny. Ha ha. Also Midge had her baby Thursday but you can forget about those booties I wouldn't let you send because the baby was born dead. See, they wouldn't have done any good anyway.

" 'Peggy sends her love. I told her you were fine and we'd see her in the fall. I know you'd like that.

" 'Remember, keep mum about everything and don't write to anybody because I don't want anything to spoil this deal. Burn this letter even. Love, H.' "

Wilks said, when he'd finished, "That Henry's a sweet boy. Mrs. K fell off the porch, ha ha. The baby was born dead. Serves you right for wanting to send a present."

"Or," Fellows added, " 'Let's make love one last time before I strangle you.' "

"Yeah," Wilks said bitterly. "Good old Henry. Anyway, he tells us a little bit for a change. I'd guess Peggy is Betty's sister and Ernie's a kid brother. That Mrs. K would be a neighbor and Midge is probably somebody she grew up with."

"They both grew up with," Fellows corrected. "Henry must have lived in the neighborhood too."

"I'll buy that. The only trouble is, what neighborhood? What city? If we knew that much we could trace Midge through the baby who died."

"Peggy was 'in' for a show," Fellows said thoughtfully. "In from where? Pittsfield perhaps?"

"Why Pittsfield?"

The chief shrugged. "I don't know, except Pittsfield keeps cropping up. I think it might be worth our while to check on infant deaths right here. And something else, too. I let Crouch stop too soon. He quit searching for a Henry Cooper when we found the house he rented, but the letters he wrote are post-marked here. If he was living in this city while he was separated from Betty it would be because his girlfriend also lived here. He either met her after he and Betty rented the house or, perhaps, he met her earlier and she's the reason he brought Betty here in the first place. If so, the chances are he still lives here. In any case, I'm going to pick up that search for quarters rented to a Henry Cooper again."

Wilks nodded. "I think you're right. He may not have grown up here but I'll lay odds he's still living here."

Fellows went after the fourth letter then. It was dated August fifth and was of no help for it consisted of a few brief sentences saying money was enclosed, the deal was prospering and should be concluded soon. At the end there was the inevitable request to destroy the letter.

"Well," Fellows said, stuffing the letters in his pocket, "no matter. She's given us a couple of tips anyway by saving these." He moved back to the suitcases. "Let's see what else she can tell us."

CHAPTER XXIV

The two men searched through the suitcases, item by item, for half an hour and then had Mike bring down the garment bags and everything else, including the television set. They were meticulous and thorough but the results were meager. There was no dealer's name on the TV and while some of the clothing had labels, they came from chain store outlets rather than exclusive shops and there was little chance they could be traced. The suitcases themselves were standard types and could have been purchased at any department store.

"Well," Wilks said, looking at the heap of clothing piled in disarray on the truck, "I think our best bet is to hunt for Cooper in Pittsfield and see if the baby died here too. I don't think there's a chance of tracing this stuff."

"I think we have an even better bet, Sid. I'd estimate you could get three to four hundred bucks from a secondhand dealer for all these things. If Henry would swipe the watch from her body I can't see him letting this stuff go by the boards. He'll be in here to collect it. You wait and see."

"It wouldn't hurt to keep an eye on 44 Glenwood Road either,

Fred. That's still his place. It wouldn't make a bad honeymoon cottage for that matter."

"Yeah, by all means. And we'll have all this sent to the lab. They might be able to trace some of it. You never can tell."

They went down in the elevator then and told Gorman that the police would collect Mrs. Cooper's belongings and stressed to him again that he was to notify headquarters the moment anybody came to get them.

When they walked out of the building a light rain was starting but it failed to dampen Fellows' spirits. "I think we'll have our man pretty soon now, Sid. A few days at the most."

Wilks wasn't quite as cheerful as the chief. He sniffed the rain distastefully and said, "I only wonder why he hasn't collected that stuff already. Presumably he knows where it is. Maybe he's scared."

Fellows refused to worry about that and the bright prospects ahead made him garrulous. "That 'Peggy' letter interests me," he said. "Did you notice that Henry hardly gives Betty the time of day in the other letters? He tells her what he wants her to do and nothing else. Here he's trying to please her, give her a few tidbits of news. I think it's because Peggy found him with another woman and he's afraid Peggy will tell. He beats her to the punch and eases a guilty conscience with the other stuff."

"That would have to mean Peggy has contact with Betty, knows her whereabouts and what she's up to."

"If Peggy's a sister that wouldn't be unlikely."

"No, but it'd be unlikely for Henry to strangle Betty if Peggy knows where they are and what's going on."

"She wouldn't have to know more than their most recent address. She wouldn't need to know the different names Betty goes under. 'Care of Mrs. Cooper' would do it. Besides, if Mrs. K had her fall a month before Betty heard about it, the contact would be very slight."

"Pretty damned slight if you ask me. There's nothing in her things that shows Betty had contact with anybody but Henry."

"Maybe she only saves Henry's letters."

Wilks laughed. "O.K., you win. They're sisters and they swap letters once in a while."

"There's more to it than that, as I see it. For instance, I think the woman Henry was with when he ran into Peggy is the girl he wants to marry. You notice how he painted her in the letter?"

"Painted her? He hardly mentioned her."

"That's right. He played her down. She's somebody he's cooking up a deal with and that's all. I think that was to give Betty the idea this woman wasn't much to look at. Remember, Henry's habit appears to be to play up to the older women and con money out of them. Betty obviously knew this and put up with it. So his letter suggests that the woman he was in the New York restaurant with is another of the same."

"And maybe she was."

"Except, if he's afraid Peggy will tell on him it's not the same setup he's been going in for in the past. This girl would be young and good-looking."

"And there's no deal in the works?"

"Sure there was a deal in the works. It was to deal Betty out. I'll lay odds the girl he was with, wittingly or unwittingly, was the cause of the divorce talk that ended up with Henry leaving the house."

Wilks laughed. "Brother, you sure do read between the lines."

"Furthermore, Henry must be serious about this girl. I mean marriage-serious. I'd figure then that it's a good bet she's not only young and pretty but she has money. Henry, seeing Betty isn't going to give him the divorce, decides to kill her. This new girl, most likely, doesn't know he's got a wife. So, for Henry, killing is easier than divorce anyway. So he starts a campaign to make Betty think he's changed his mind and all will be peachy."

"Some campaign. 'Do this', 'do that' and if you behave yourself I might let you have a baby."

"He doesn't have to step out of character and sweet-talk her. The testimony's all been that she was very much in love with him. She'd take whatever he dished out and do whatever he told her to rather than risk losing him."

Wilks grinned. "Maybe what you really mean is she was *loyal* to him."

Fellows gave him a twisted smile. "If you insist, we'll say she was loyal."

"Which is what I've been saying right along. She's not helping him in his little adventures. She goes along with him because her only other choice is to leave him and this she won't do if he kills her for it."

"Have it your way. Only this time he's afraid she might not be so willing to go along. This time it's different. So he tries to stall off any trouble by writing the 'Peggy' letter. He's setting Betty up for the slaughter and he doesn't want her to kick over the traces. How does that sound?"

"It sounds great for a theory but frankly, Fred, I'm only interested in hearing about five things that have to do with fact."

"Which are?"

"The alarm we've got out for his Volkswagen, the watch we're going to set up on his bungalow, the watch on that storage company, the hunt for a rent in Henry Cooper's name, and a check through the Pittsfield records for a baby who was born dead on the last Thursday in July."

CHAPTER XXV

All of Betty's belongings, except the letters and pictures, were shipped to the lab the following day as a matter of routine. From the lab would come the subtle bits of evidence, the analysis of dust and stains that might show where she'd been and what she'd done. From there the tracing would start, the attempt to locate which shipment of garments hers had come from, to what store they had gone and when. When had her suitcases been manufactured and where had they been purchased?

Tracing a person's background through these methods were, however, long time operations. This was the kind of work that turned up murderers years after their crime had been forgotten by the public and nearly forgotten by themselves. This was the sort of dogged work that produced the lightning bolt from the skies, the sudden policeman's hand on the shoulder of a man who had long since believed he had got away free.

Fred Fellows, on the other hand, had no expectation that this would be such a case. Even when Ed Lewis reported that insurance companies had never found a trace of either the stolen jewels or the thief, even when a check of infant mortalities in Pittsfield produced a blank, he was still convinced it wouldn't take long to track the man down. Those disappointments meant little when there were so many hot leads to follow.

Fellows' optimism received a severe jolt, however, on Wednesday, the second of October. That was the day the Pittsfield police completed their search for Henry's living quarters and reported failure. Every motel, hotel, rooming house, every landlord and real estate agent in the city and its surrounding suburbs had been contacted and the only rent to a Henry Cooper was the house at 44 Glenwood Road. Either he had changed his name again or he was no longer in Pittsfield.

This was a bitter disappointment to the Stockford chief and the disappointment grew greater with each passing day. By the time Pittsfield reported late Friday afternoon that still no one had come to the Cooper house, that no one had showed up at the Van Moter Company and that no Volkswagen with the plates AM99874 had been spotted, he was growing desperate.

"Sid," he said, "we must be doing something wrong. We must have got off the track somewhere. Why hasn't he showed up to claim Betty's things? It's the fourth of October and they were only paid for through the thirtieth. Why does he still stay away from the house? Why hasn't his car been seen?"

Wilks, slumped in a chair in the chief's office, bit off a piece of tobacco and said, "The most likely answer is that he's left town."

"Leaving a television set and all those other things behind?"

"If he's hooked up with another girl and that girl doesn't know about Betty, all those dresses and shoes and stuff might be hard to explain. And if that girl has money, what does he care about an extra three or four hundred dollars?"

"But if he left town, where would he go? The alarm for that car is out all over the East."

"If he left town he probably left with the girl and she might have a nicer car. My guess is his Volkswagen is sitting in a garage somewhere."

Fellows rubbed a hand over his face. "I'm going to have to reorient my thinking." He dug through the papers on his desk and picked up the snapshot of the young man in bathing trunks. "There's his picture, God damn it. He *does* exist. Sometimes I begin to wonder." He tossed the picture back. "A case where somebody gets murdered," he said, "where there are no clues and you just have no idea who did it, that's one thing. But to have a murder case where you're damned sure you know the killer but you can't find him, that gets me."

"He's pretty slick at disconnecting himself from the past," Wilks agreed. "He appears and then disappears, then reappears somewhere else as somebody else. A guy like that's going to be hard to catch because you can't follow him. All you can do is anticipate him and try to be there when he appears. My guess is we aren't going to get anything on those leads we've been following. If it hasn't happened by this time it probably won't at all. What I think is he's taken off with this new girl and they're starting a new life somewhere else—probably under any name but Cooper or Moore."

"You're probably right," the chief said dismally. "That's the hell of it. You're probably right about the anticipation business too. The trouble is, you can't anticipate somebody if you don't know anything about him." He sighed. "I can't spare the manpower very well but it looks as though we'll have to go back to that stillborn child he mentioned in the 'Peggy' letter."

"Try to trace the woman?"

"That's right. Every child who died before or right after birth between July twentieth and twenty-fifth in every town and city within a seventy-five mile radius of Times Square. We'll collect the names of every woman involved and show them Betty's picture. If we can get the local police forces to help that will save my own men and, more important, save one hell of a lot of time. Anyway, that's something, I guess, that's got to be done."

"New York City too?"

"You bet New York City too. Peggy could have come 'in' for the show from Brooklyn, the Bronx, Queens, or Staten Island and we won't overlook Manhattan either. I'm not going to overlook a damned thing because I want to turn up that 'Midge' woman."

"You want me to set the thing up, Fred?"

"No, because there's one other line to follow. Henry wanted to marry this girl, whoever she is. If he killed Betty so he could, then maybe he already has. What you're going to do is check into every marriage in Pittsfield from September first on. Henry may be in there somewhere under some kind of a name."

Wilks nodded. "It's very likely. Between that and the hunt for Midge we might pick up a trail."

"Let's hope. If not, then we'll have to pray Peggy writes to Betty at that Glenwood Road address sometime soon to tattle on Henry."

CHAPTER XXVI

It took Wilks five days of intensive work in the Hall of Records in Pittsfield and out in the field making phone calls and ringing doorbells to determine that Henry, more of a phantom than ever, had not married anyone in that city aftèr the death of his earlier wife. In that same period of time all garages, parking lots and other possible storage spots in Pittsfield, Stockford and every other of the dozen towns in Pittsfield County were searched in vain for the missing Volkswagen. Henry had apparently not only disappeared but had left no trace of his earlier presence other than the body he had abandoned on the beach.

By the time those lines of investigation had petered out the list of women bearing stillborn children late in July had been assembled and the business of contacting them was under way. Police departments in all the localities helped in the task and in the following two days every woman over an area of forty thousand square miles who had lost a baby in birth two and a half months before was shown a picture of Betty. One after another the reports came in with the inevitable answer. The woman did not know the girl.

"That lousy liar," Wilks was goaded to remark as his desperation grew. "I'll bet Midge's baby never died at all. I'll bet that's just one more of his stories!" For him the hunt for Henry was turning into a personal vendetta and his frustration was intense. "The idea," he complained bitterly, "that that punk can date a girl for two hours and not be seen with her, that he can murder her on a public beach and get away, that he can walk by another couple and get described and not get caught, that he can leave the girl's body out in plain sight on the sand and disappear, this gets me. We know two of his aliases, we have his picture, we have his handwriting. We know places he's been, we know houses he's rented, people he's talked to. We know the make and license number of his car, the jewelry he stole, the clothes and things his wife owned. We've got everything but his fingerprints—hell, we even have a piece of one of those—and we still can't find him. If I believed in ghosts, I'd believe he was one. But I don't believe in ghosts and that means he isn't one and I don't like the idea that he can stand around thumbing his nose at us."

Fellows felt the frustration too, though he was less vocal about it. Ironclad lead after ironclad lead had led to nowhere. His most certain deductions had turned out false, the most promising clues gave wrong answers. Even the few breaks that had resulted from painstaking effort didn't really break anything at all. The man called Henry was either incredibly smart or incredibly lucky.

Even before the final report turned the hunt for Midge into failure Fellows had abandoned hope in that direction and Thursday night and Friday he took the case file home with him, poring over it in a search for some new direction to follow. It seemed that every possibility had already been explored but, like Wilks, he was feeling personally flaunted and he was reluctant to acknowledge failure.

CHAPTER XXVII

At half past nine that Friday evening, the eleventh of October, Fellows made another visit to Wilks' cellar where the detective sergeant kept his spread of model trains. Wilks, who spent more time assembling the models and monkeying with them than he ever did running them, was, as usual, busy with his tools. The trains were his therapy and thoughts of Handsome Henry and Beautiful Betty could be put away. "Here comes the chief," he said without looking up. "Don't you ever stay home?"

Fellows, coming off the steps and crossing the floor, said, "I've heard of grass widows and golf widows but your wife is the first train widow I've ever known. I'll bet you don't even remember what she looks like."

"Oh, we get together at times. Now and then there's something on television that doesn't have to do with crime and I'll go up and watch it with her."

"A baseball game you mean?"

"And we eat breakfast together and sometimes, on those few occasions when you don't make me work overtime, we get to have dinner together."

"Well, of course I'll admit you're easier to live with locked away in the cellar. I always did wonder how she stood you all these years."

Wilks turned around slowly. "Say, you don't have Henry up your sleeve, do you? All this repartee doesn't become a frustrated chief of police."

"No," Fellows said, hitching a hip onto the edge of the worktable. "I wish it was that easy."

"You're onto something. You're not here to tell me there's nothing in the files."

"I've been racking my brains. Maybe that's my trouble. I think I'm getting softheaded."

"What have you been racking them about?"

"The 'Peggy' letter."

"That thing again, or still? You read three fathoms deep between the lines the day you found it. How deep have you gone now?"

"Six fathoms."

"You're wasting your time. That letter's a mare's nest."

"That letter," Fellows said, "is the only piece of Henry we've got. It's the only place where he let's himself go at all. Everywhere else he's a cipher but there he reveals himself a little."

"He reveals himself as a liar. Midge and her stillborn baby! I'll bet Mrs. K never fell off the porch either."

"I'll tell you, Sid, I don't think he made that up about the baby. I think Midge did lose her baby."

"Not within seventy-five miles of New York she didn't. What are you going to do, try for a hundred?"

"I don't think that would turn her up and I should have seen it before. The point is this. Midge grows up with Henry and Betty and Peggy, sure, but Midge is now married. Why should we assume she still lives in the neighborhood she grew up in? She could be living in Chicago or California now. Peggy wouldn't have had to learn about the baby from Midge, she could have learned about it from Midge's mother. It would be the *mother* who'd still live in the same old neighborhood, see? And if the mother was around to tell Peggy about the dead baby instead of being with her daughter wherever she was having it, then the daughter must be living too far away to make the trip feasible. I think it highly unlikely, therefore, that the dead child was born within a hundred mile radius of New York."

Wilks put his hands on his hips. "Is that what you've been doing the past couple of days, figuring out how Midge could have had her baby outside the seventy-five mile limit? Is that what you came over here to tell me?"

"Well hardly."

"Well hardly, I should hope so. Even if your conclusion is right, what the hell good does that do us?"

"That's just a little sidelight I thought you might be interested in," Fellows said. "No, that's not what I came over for but what I did come over for isn't much better."

"It can't be much worse. What is it?"

"I'm afraid to tell you."

"Why?"

"This is so far out in the stratosphere it's even too far out for me."

Wilks shrugged. "If you're afraid to tell me, I'm afraid to listen. But go ahead. I'll grit my teeth and bear it."

"First I want to ask you a few questions. I want you to tell me about Betty. You say she's not a sinner, she's a saint. How much of a saint?"

Wilks eyed the chief querulously. "Does that have something to do with this?"

"I'm looking for support. You say she's loyal. What else?"

"Virtuous. I wish I knew what the hell you're driving at."

"Kind or cruel?"

"Kind, naturally."

"In the 'Peggy' letter, Henry laughs at Mrs. K falling off the stoop and getting two black eyes. We both agree this shows what kind of a guy *he* is. But, remember, he chooses to tell this as a joke to Betty. What does that make her?"

"She wouldn't think it was funny."

"Then why would he tell it to her as a joke if he didn't think she'd appreciate it as a joke?"

"Because," Wilks answered, "Henry is totally self-centered. He doesn't give a damn what Betty thinks. He probably didn't even know what she thought or felt, much less care. You said in that letter he was trying to be chatty. He did it *his* way."

"So you don't think Betty would laugh at his little joke?"

"Hell, no. If a man slipped on a banana peel, Henry would laugh but Betty would run to help him up. That's the way I see her." He looked at Fellows. "I suppose you don't?"

"Oh, no, Sid. You've pretty well won me over. I go your way now. So let's go a little farther. It's your feeling that Betty was anxious to settle down and raise a family?"

"It's not just my feeling, that's the testimony."

"That's right. She was crazy about babies according to Mrs. Sears. How do you figure she would feel then when she hears that Midge's baby was stillborn?"

"Very sorry."

"Do you think her regret at Midge's misfortune would be strong enough for her to offer some kind of consolation?"

"Yes, certainly."

"Strong enough for her to do that despite the fact that Henry ordered her not to get in touch with anybody?"

Wilks eyed the chief carefully. "You *are* getting out in the stratosphere aren't you?"

"You ain't heard nothing yet. But answer the question."

"I think she might. But what if she did? Let her send a card or something and what good does it do us? That's not going to tell us where she sent it."

"That's right. If she sent a card or a letter it wouldn't."

"Come on, come on," said Wilks impatiently. "Lay off the suspense, will you?"

"All right. One more question. Do you think she might send flowers?"

That brought Wilks to a dead stop. "So that's what you have up your sleeve," he said finally. "I don't know, Fred. I don't know. I'm not that sure of what goes on in a woman's mind. She might have, I suppose. It's a long, long, long shot but it wouldn't hurt to find out."

"That's the way I look at it," the chief said. "And maybe we're due for a break. All our ironclad leads have come to dead ends. Maybe a flight of fancy will get us a different answer."

"She didn't have a phone," Wilks reflected, "and Mrs. Sears didn't mention her ever asking to use hers. Probably she'd have had to go to a florists' shop directly, or maybe Western Union."

Fellows nodded. "I've copied down the names of all the florists in Pittsfield and have checked them on a map. The nearest one is the Hampton Florist Shop on Union Avenue and it would be in the shopping district where Betty would go to get her provisions."

Wilks brightened at that. "Seeing that florist shop every time she went to market might give her the idea. When do we go?"

"First thing tomorrow morning. And when you go to sleep tonight, don't forget your prayers."

CHAPTER XXVIII

The shopping district which included the Hampton Florist Shop was a brief series of stores on both sides of Union Avenue only two blocks from Glenwood Road. There was an A&P, a delicatessen, liquor store, fruit store, bakery shop, dry cleaners, real estate office, and drug store in addition to the florists'. Fellows had a brief pang coming into Pittsfield when he saw preparations for the Columbus Day parade for he had totally forgotten it was a holiday. To his relief, however, though several other establishments were closed, Hampton's was doing business.

The shop, a cramped space crowded with greenery, smelled moist and fresh. A slight man with a large nose and an ethereal air came out from an inner room in shirt sleeves and dark trousers. "Yes?" he said, staring first at the chief's uniform and then at Wilks' suit. "You want flowers?" he asked, turning back to the chief in disbelief.

"We'd like some information about flowers," the chief said. "Do you wire them?"

"Yes. We do that."

"Would you have records of any flowers sent or wired on July twenty-ninth or thirtieth?"

"Yes. I have those records. Do you want to know whom flowers were sent to or who sent them?"

"Both. I want to know if a Mrs. Henry Cooper sent any on either of those days."

"Mrs. Henry Cooper? July twenty-ninth or thirtieth? That should be easy." He went into a tiny office containing a desk and chair and flipped open a black leather book lying on the blotter. He found the page and ran a finger down the names. "No," he said. "Nothing from a Mrs. Henry Cooper."

"Try the whole week from July twenty-eighth through August fourth."

The man went swiftly through the list, flipped a page and stopped halfway down the column. "No. No such woman, sir."

Wilks sighed with resignation. "Well, it was a long shot."

"Wait a minute," Fellows interrupted. "Your girlfriend uses all kinds of names. How about somebody named Moore?"

The man went through the whole procedure again. "No, sir. Nobody named Moore."

Fellows went into the office with him and bent over the book himself. "Anybody named Henry or Betty wire flowers during this time?"

The man was beginning to tire. He sighed and started once more. "On the twenty-ninth of July there was an order sent by a Mrs. Betty Larkin. On the thirtieth, there's a Henry Buxhall—"

"Wait a minute. Not so fast. What's Mrs. Betty Larkin's address?"

"Let's see, uh, 37 Dearwood Place."

"Did you bill her or did she pay cash?"

"I've got it marked here that she paid cash."

"Did she send a note with the flowers?"

"Probably but I don't keep records of the notes more than a week."

"All right. May I see a phone book?"

The florist pulled that from the drawer and Fellows handed it out to Wilks. "Check on her, will you? Now next there's a Henry Buxhall?"

"Yes, sir. 88 Maple Street."

"Any others?"

Wilks stopped thumbing pages and peered close. "There's no Larkin on Dearwood Place."

"O.K., check Buxhall." Fellows turned to the florist. "Where's Dearwood Place? Do you know?"

"I never heard of it," the man said. "I can look it up on the map."

Fellows followed the florist into an even moister back room and Wilks came behind saying, "Buxhall. 88 Maple. He's there."

They waited while the man looked through the guide of the

map folder. He double-checked and frowned. "Well I don't understand it," he said at last. "There isn't any Dearwood Place listed. Maybe it's a new road."

"Maybe it doesn't even exist," Fellows replied. "Now will you let me have the name and address of the person the flowers were sent to?"

Back the man went to the office and his book, Fellows, lingering outside, said to Wilks, "I'll lay you odds that's her real name. She couldn't use an alias sending flowers to an old friend so she made up the address."

The florist came out with a slip of paper. "It's a Mrs. Margaret Hallock, 642 Warner Street in Washington, D.C. Here, I've got it all written down."

Fellows verified the paper and nodded grimly. "Thanks very much." He turned to Wilks. "We'll check this out from Crouch's office. No point wasting time going back to Stockford."

The florist said, "Have I helped you gentlemen?"

"A great deal," Fellows told him. "You may have just broken a murder case for us." He walked out with Wilks while the man stared after them open-mouthed.

CHAPTER XXIX

045   FILE 1   PD PITTSFIELD CT   OCT 12-63
PD WASHINGTON DC
REQUEST INFO GIRL MURDER VICTIM PICTURE ON WIRE SHOW TO
MRS MARGARET HALLOCK 642 WARNER ST UR CITY WANT IDENTI-
FICATION RUSH PLEASE CONFIRM
AUTH   A G CROUCH   OPR MACDADE   9-55 AM
ZZZZZ

082   FILE 10   PD WASHINGTON DC   OCT 12-63
PD PITTSFIELD CT
PICTURE RECD WILL COMPLY IMMED
AUTH   P C HARRIGAN   OPR SISSON   10-10 AM
ZZZZZ

Fellows and Wilks did not go out for lunch at noon. They
had a sandwich brought in for they wanted to be right there
each time the teletype machine in the communications room
of the Pittsfield Police Department started clicking. "We act
like a couple of amateurs," Fellows said wryly. "You'd think
we'd never asked for a report before."

"A lot hangs on this one," Wilks said. "Let's face it."

"The trouble is we get too involved."

"Are we supposed to apologize for that? Is there some virtue
in not giving a damn? So let the cops around here think we're
crazy or small-time. I liked the looks of that girl who was killed
and I wouldn't feel happy if the guy who did it got off free."

Fellows looked at his watch. "If by 'immediately' Washington means right then and not sometime today, they've had two
hours. Of course, if the woman wasn't home—"

He was interrupted by the sudden clacking of the machine
and both leaped to see, then returned to their chairs. The message
had nothing to do with Pittsfield.

Their sandwiches and coffee arrived and when they were finishing the meal, Crouch stuck his head in to see if there was
word. Told no, he said, "Well, of course they got their own
business. It's not their murder."

The machine started chattering again and the three went to
watch and read as it spelled out:

082   FILE 10   PD WASHINGTON DC   OCT 12-63
PD PITTSFIELD CT
PIC IDENTIFIED BETTY LARKIN NEE WILLIAMS LAST KNOWN 37
DEARWOOD PLACE UR TOWN RAISED 1438 16TH AVE BRONX NY WITH
MOTHER SISTER 2 BROTHERS MARRIED HENRY LARKIN 1464 17TH
AVE BRONX NY 1957 WHEREABOUTS UNKNOWN THEREAFTER EX-

CEPT RETURN FOR MOTHER'S FUNERAL 1961 PLEASE CONFIRM
AUTH   P C HARRIGAN   OPR SISSON   12-43 PM
ZZZZZ

Wilks tore the message from the machine with glee. "We've got him. That's my Betty. She disobeyed her husband on two things. She saved his letters and she sent out flowers. She was his slave but she had the moral fiber to balk when he asked too much and that's going to hang the bastard."

Fellows smiled but it was a sober smile. "We've found where he comes from but don't forget, that's not where he *is*."

"Since when is it your turn to be the wet blanket? This is *one* past he can't totally sever connections with."

"This should help," Fellows admitted, "but don't count on its being the whole thing."

"Well, let's get an investigation started and see. Let's get hold of the New York police."

Fellows rubbed his chin. "I was rather thinking of going down there myself."

Wilks laughed. "Oh. Doesn't mean a thing, does it? Only you think you'll go down there in person, huh? Well let's get going."

CHAPTER XXX

The section of 17th Avenue where Henry Larkin had lived was a rundown slum with grimy-windowed shops, blackened tenements and broken cobblestone streets. Little girls in soiled cotton dresses played hopscotch on cracked sidewalks and older girls, in neater clothes, gathered on stone stoops to gab with each other and tease with the boys. There were pungent smells of indeterminate origin, unpleasing without being unpleasant. On the side streets there was stickball and in one place a youth batted a wornout tennis ball against a brick wall with a racket.

1464 17th Avenue was a narrow four-story building with brownstone steps and iron railings and Fellows, Wilks and a young New York detective named Joe Finney climbed the steps and entered the vestibule at four o'clock that afternoon. The name "Larkin, Mrs. H." was on the mailbox for apartment 2A and the three men went up a flight and found the door opposite the next staircase.

There was nothing but silence after the first ring but a second brought creaking sounds from inside and a muttered, "All right, all right." The door was pulled open and the three detectives found themselves staring at a mountain of a woman who stood at least five nine and whose three hundred odd pounds of flesh was covered by a faded blue print dress that looked like a tent. She stared back, poking her scraggly gray hair with banana-like fingers and said, "What the hell's this?"

Finney was the one who enlightened her. "Police," he said, showing his badge. He confirmed that she was Mrs. H. Larkin and said they'd like to talk.

Mrs. Larkin made a face. "I don't know what there is to talk about," she said but she let them in.

The door opened into the parlor which overlooked the street and the furnishings there were better than expected. The lace curtains, like the shapeless dress, were sparkling clean as were the antimacassars which decorated the carefully kept overstuffed chairs and couch. The rug was worn from many sweepings but the sweepings kept it dustless.

The huge woman waddled to the couch in front of the windows and took hold with both hands when she sat down, the action bringing a heavy creak of protest from the springs. Fellows, Wilks and Finney took other chairs and Fellows leaned forward to give the woman the inevitable picture of Betty. "Do you know this girl?" he asked and his tone was that of a man wanting a piece of inconsequential information. His plan of campaign was to avoid frightening Henry's mother into silence by suggesting her son might have done something wrong.

Mrs. Larkin hesitated and the hesitation said she did though her face showed nothing. "What's this about?" she asked warily, not answering the question.

"We're trying to find out something about this girl and we understand—"

"What's she done?"

Fellows smiled disarmingly. "Nothing. At least not to our knowledge."

"Then what do you want with her?"

"Nothing. We're trying to find her next of kin."

That brought an immediate response. The woman's eyes widened in alarm. "What's happened to her? What's the matter?"

Fellows was very sober. "She's had a serious accident. We're trying to notify—"

"What kind of accident? How bad?"

"Pretty bad, I'm afraid. We're trying to find somebody who knows her—"

"What about my son?" she asked in even greater alarm. "Is he all right?"

"Her husband?"

"Yes. What about him?"

"We don't know where he is. We're trying to locate him to let him know."

"You mean he wasn't with her? He doesn't know about it?"

"That seems to be the case. That's why we've come to you. We thought you could tell us where we could reach him."

"Me?" She shrugged her huge shoulders, the alarm still on her face. "I don't know where he is. I don't understand this."

"When did you last hear from him?"

"I ain't heard from him. He ain't the letter-writing kind. But what's about the accident? What's with Betty? Why wasn't he there?"

"Don't you have any idea where he might be?"

"Me? Hell, he'd be with her, wouldn't he? You sure he wasn't with her? Maybe he was in it. Maybe he was h-hurt—."

"He wasn't in it," Fellows insisted. "He wasn't hurt. Please try to think. We've got to contact him."

She shook her head distractedly. "I don't know nothing," she said. "I only seen him once since him and Betty left here. They come by when her ma died, after the funeral. They didn't stay long." She looked in fear at the chief. "You sure he's all right? You sure he's not hurt?"

"We think so. But we can't be sure if we can't find him."

Mrs. Larkin clapped her hands together, prayer fashion, and gazed upward reverently. "God wouldn't be that mean. God wouldn't hurt a nice boy like my Henry." She looked at Fellows again. "But Betty. How did it happen to Betty? Tell me what happened."

Fellows sticking to the truth as much as possible, explained that Betty had been attacked by robbers. She had been badly hurt.

Mrs. Larkin leaned forward, her mouth slack. "What about her? How bad is it? She's gonna be all right, ain't she?"

Fellows shook his head slowly. "I'm afraid not, Mrs. Larkin."

"You mean she's—?" Mrs. Larkin read the confirmation in the chief's face and started to weep. She pulled a handkerchief from the pocket of her housedress and held it with both hands to her eyes. "Oh, my poor Betty," she moaned. "Loved her like a daughter, I did."

The policemen remained quiet for a bit while the woman wept. Then she said in muffled tones, "Such a sweet girl, such a hard life. Oh, my poor Henry. He adored her so."

Fellows took that opportunity to say gently, "Could you tell us about her, Mrs. Larkin? We're trying to find out as much as we can. It might help us catch the robber."

She lifted red-rimmed eyes from the handkerchief. "You think it would?"

"Yes. Would you help us?"

She nodded faintly. "A sweet girl," she said. "I can tell you that. You ask me, I'll tell you." She blew her nose on the handkerchief and it sounded like a gun going off.

150   THE MISSING MAN

Fellows got out his notebook. "You liked her for a daughter-in-law, I take it?"

Mrs. Larkin's eyes filmed with tears. "Nice as they come," she whispered. "She had a hard life but she turned out a good girl."

"What kind of a hard life?"

"Very hard. She had a no-good father and a no-good mother, she did. The old man ran off with another woman and ditched them all when Betty was a kid. Twelve years old, she was, with no father and a souse for a mother. Her ma was a souse but the old man shouldn't've left her. He shouldn't've left four kids to an old souse. Drank herself into her grave, her ma did, and Betty came back to the funeral. She didn't owe her that. She didn't owe her ma a thing."

"Who took care of the family after the father deserted it?"

"That was Betty," Mrs. Larkin said simply and wiped her eyes. "She kept the family together. She did it even before the old man left but more after. It was her did the housework and minded the other kids."

"What about money? How did they eat?"

"Relief money. That's what it was. They were on relief. There was talk about putting the children in a home, what with her pa gone and her ma doing nothing but drink, but Betty had the spunk and she told them people she could manage the house and, with the help of the Lord, she did, too. Them relief people, they give the money to Betty so her ma wouldn't drink it up and she brought up the kids real good. That Peggy, she's turned out a real fine girl. Real fine. The two boys too—Ernie and Keith."

Fellows said, "How old was Betty when she married your son?"

"Sixteen she was, with my boy twenty."

"They were pretty young, then."

"Hell, they were old enough. They'd've got married sooner except Betty wouldn't leave the house till Peggy was old enough to run it. Her ma, of course, kicked and screamed. She didn't want her leaving, but that old souse was lucky Betty stuck it out as long as she did. That was no life for a young girl."

"Did you favor the marriage?"

Mrs. Larkin snorted. "Favor it? I couldn't wait to see them get hitched. You should've seen some of the tramps my Henry went with before he took up with Betty. I got nightmares thinking about his marrying one of them. Her ma, though, she wouldn't give permission and it's a good thing they eloped. The way they were stuck on each other it's a cinch they'd've got in trouble if they hadn't got hitched. That way they were honest and decent."

Fellows asked what they'd done after the marriage and Mrs. Larkin said they took a room in the neighborhood to start with. "Henry had a job as a busboy in a fancy restaurant and Betty was a waitress in a diner. It was a struggle, just starting out, but my boy—they don't come no better than my Henry—he wasn't going to be struggling all his life. He had brains and looks and charm, Henry did. He had manners like you don't see around here. Even as a kid he had manners. They come to him natural."

Her face glowed with a certain contented pride. "Well, it didn't surprise me none," she went on, "but those people he waited on took a shine to him. What would you expect with him so good-looking and elegant mannered and all? Some of those rich women came to the restaurant, they put him on some stock transactions or something and after a few months he had a big windfall. I didn't understand it when he explained it to me, but he made quite a bit of money."

"And he stopped being a busboy?"

Mrs. Larkin nodded. "You can say that again. He quit that job and him and Betty moved to New Jersey, down Princeton way and Henry got another job. It was a better one, something somebody'd put him onto, he told me, and then he got outside work or something. I never knew quite what because he never wrote and Betty didn't write much and didn't explain it much, but they did very well there and then they moved again. It was something about a transfer which I didn't quite understand, and after that I lost track of them. Like I say, Betty didn't write much.

"Of course, once in a while she'd write, say like around Christmas, and say things were going all right and they were happy and pretty soon they'd be settling back in one place and then she could give me an address so I could write back."

Fellows frowned. "She never had return addresses on her letters? There was no way you could write to them?"

"Nope. Well, once in a while she had them, I remember, when they were in one spot long enough. I'm no letter-writer myself, though, so it didn't matter, except when her ma was ill and dying I wrote them and I guess Peggy wrote her about it and they came back for the funeral. They were out somewhere in Ohio that time."

"Do you happen to have the letters she wrote?"

"Me?" Mrs. Larkin snorted. "What would I want them for? You read them, you've read them."

"What about Peggy? Do you think she kept hers?"

"She might've. I don't know. I don't have much contact."

"And Betty never told you what sort of work Henry was doing?"

"Not exactly, except that it was something that kept him moving around a lot. They were in boarding houses some, I recall, and on the road a lot. I think it was some kind of selling. Henry was a born salesman. He was so handsome and sincere and he had a wonderful personality."

Fellows said, "They must have made a fine-looking couple." He reached over and picked up the photo of Betty. "She was certainly a pretty thing. Do you have any pictures of Henry?"

"Just his graduation photo from high school, taken back in 1955. You want to see it?"

"I'd like to very much."

That pleased her and she wrestled and struggled and finally managed to get herself off the couch. She waddled slowly past the chief and into a back room, returning with a portrait in a black frame. She handed it to Fellows and went through the arduous process of letting herself down onto the couch cushions again.

The youth in the picture was unmistakably handsome with his black wavy hair combed just so and his ready smile. There was a slightly rakish air about him too which added to his charm. Fellows studied the portrait thoughtfully, passed it around to Wilks and Finney, took it back and studied it some more. "Colter Studio," he observed. "Well, he's certainly as good-looking a male as Betty was a female."

"And doing right well for himself," Mrs. Larkin added. "Which is only proper. A boy like him deserved the better things in life. If only—." Her eyes filled with tears again. "If only he's all right. Now Betty's dead. My poor boy."

"He ever send money home?" Fellows asked to distract her sadness.

"No," she said, not quite liking the question. "But that's because I don't need none. I got my old man's pension and that does me just fine. Henry needed his money for him and Betty so they could save up and settle down." She sniffed and reached for her handkerchief. "And now she's gone. Now Betty's gone."

"And you've only seen him once since they left here?" Fellows asked pointedly. "Don't you miss him?"

A shadow crossed her face but only for a moment and she shrugged. "Well, you know, who wants to be tied down to the old lady? It's not like they were living in the neighborhood. When they were I saw them lots. But he's been going all over the place all the time and he can't stop and make a trip from some faraway place all the way to New York just to see me." She grew sad again. "Of course, now that Betty's gone, he'll come back again. When he knows she's gone he'll come home. I was always the one he come to when he got hurt."

Fellows picked up the photo of Henry and studied it again. "I wonder if we could borrow this," he said.

That brought her up sharply. "No sirree, Bub. You don't take that picture. That's the only one I got of my boy and that don't leave these premises."

"We just want to make copies of it to help us find him. We'd return it of course."

"Nope. Absolutely not. That's all I got of my boy and that stays put."

Fellows put the picture down regretfully and got up to leave.

Mrs. Larkin didn't attempt to rise from the couch but she pointed hopefully. "Say, I don't want to impose or nothing, but could I buy a copy of that picture you got of Betty? I don't have none of her and that don't seem right." Her eyes were moist and yearning. "Of course I know she's dead now but it—well— I'd kind of like one."

Fellows picked it up and handed it to her. "You may have it with our compliments," he said. "We have others."

She thanked him happily and studied it. "She sure looks nice," she said. "She's kind of older than when I knew her. Must be twenty-two going on twenty-three and Henry's only seventeen in the other one." She looked up brightly. "He's twenty-six now, had his birthday last June."

The policemen left her still on the couch looking from one picture to the other, said their goodbyes from the door and went down to the street again and the patrol car at the curb. They climbed in and Finney started off for Peggy's house. Fellows sat down in the rear seat frowning and stroking his chin. "Colter Studio. We'll get copies from them. You study that picture close, Sid? Does Henry remind you of anybody?"

"No," Wilks said without hesitation. "Should he?"

"Somehow there was something familiar about his face but I can't think who he makes me think of."

"A movie star? Farley Granger maybe?"

Fellows shook his head. "I don't think so. Maybe somebody in Pittsfield?" He mulled that over and said, "Somebody out of the past perhaps?"

"Maybe he's a type, Fred. He makes you think of somebody because you've seen other people with the same kind of face."

Fellows shrugged but remained dissatisfied. Wilks said, "Forget it. It's not somebody we've seen on the case because if we had, you can bet I'd remember."

CHAPTER XXXI

Fellows, Wilks and Finney didn't get to see Peggy Williams that day. The house was empty and neighbors said she and her brothers had gone off to visit relatives. They waited till it was clear the family wouldn't be back for supper and gave it up. Finney said he'd interview Peggy first thing in the morning and Fellows accepted that. He briefed Finney on what they wanted from the girl and Finney, who was a young, good-looking bachelor, was glad to oblige. "I just hope she looks like her sister," he said.

"I just hope," Fellows replied, "that you'll also remember to go to Colter's Studio on Monday and get some prints of Henry's picture."

They went back to precinct headquarters where Fellows cleared the plan with the captain and he and Wilks started back for Stockford. "Well," the detective sergeant said, without enthusiasm, "now we're going to get an eight year old picture of Henry to circulate. I suppose you could call that progress."

"It's a step in the right direction."

"Everything's a step in the right direction but it doesn't seem to bring us any closer to Henry."

"Also," Fellows reminded him, "Peggy saw the girl Henry was with. The chances are she'll remember her name."

"The chances are," Wilks retorted sourly, "that Henry never introduced the girl to Peggy. I certainly wouldn't." He sat back and shook his head. "I don't see where this helps us a damned bit. That picture isn't going to do us any more good than that flyer we put out about Betty's watch."

"It might if we showed it in the right places."

"All we have to do is find some right places. You got any in mind?"

Fellows nodded. "Yes, I have, Sid. I've been thinking about that and I can tell you the first place I'm going with that picture is Little Bohemia."

"I don't think that's going to do you much good. He kept out of sight."

"The night of the murder he kept out of sight. But that's not the only time he was ever there."

"So he reconnoitered the place. So you find somebody who says, 'Yeah, I saw him once.' So what?"

Fellows stopped for a light and eased his position in the seat a little. "Sid, you ever hear the story of the farmer who kept having his vegetable garden raided by skunks?"

Wilks took out his chewing tobacco and sat up. "No," he said. "I never heard the story of the farmer whose vegetable garden was being raided by skunks and I can't wait to."

Fellows shifted gears and started forward. "Well, this farmer took out his shotgun and a chair and he sat beside that garden day after day from breakfast to dinner on the lookout for skunks. Finally, one day, a friend happened by and asked what he was doing and the farmer told him. So the friend said, 'But don't you know skunks are nocturnal animals? They only come out at night?' So the farmer says, 'Sure I do but I can't come out here then. I'm afraid of the dark.'"

Wilks said, "That's a great story. That breaks me up. What's it supposed to mean?"

"I've been thinking about where that girl was killed."

"You still elude me. Henry certainly wasn't afraid of the dark. He wasn't afraid of much of anything."

"That's right. But doesn't that beach strike you as a remarkable place to commit a murder?"

"It always has."

"If you were going to strangle a girl, wouldn't you pick a different spot than that? You've got a Volkswagen. You can drive anywhere in it."

"I would. But I'm not Henry."

"What's more, Sid, isn't Little Bohemia a strange place to bring the girl to to set her up for the killing?"

"I don't know that I'd pick it. I certainly wouldn't pick the beach. What are you driving at?"

"I'm wondering if Henry might not be a little like that farmer. I'm wondering if he picks a poor spot for a murder because it's a familiar spot and he'd rather do that than pick a good spot that would be unfamiliar."

"You're reaching pretty far out into the old stratosphere, you know."

"I know. But what about the room he told her to get? In his letter he spelled out the house to go to. I grant you there were plenty of vacancies but he had to know there were vacancies at Mrs. Fremont's. Since he didn't write or call Mrs. Fremont he must have actually seen her sign."

Wilks, biting off his tobacco and tucking the packet back in his pocket, slumped in his seat and said, "Of course it's obvious he reconnoitered the place. He had to know something about the beach and what went on there and all the rest of it."

"But," persisted Fellows, "wouldn't a simple reconnoitering job cause him to look somewhere else? If I were looking for a murder spot I'd give up on the beach the moment I found other couples necked there. He didn't."

"That means something to you but I don't know just what."

"I'm wondering if perhaps he didn't actually live in Little Bohemia. That's what I mean about showing his picture around there. We've been thrown off by the Pittsfield postmarks on his letters to Betty. A Pittsfield postmark merely means the letters were mailed in Pittsfield. It doesn't necessarily mean the writer of the letters has to *live* in Pittsfield."

Wilks twisted his head to scowl at Fellows. "You mean you think he wrote letters in Little Bohemia and then drove all the way to Pittsfield to mail them? What's the point? It would have been as simple to deliver them in person."

"There are a number of points. The first is he doesn't want Betty to know where he is. Pittsfield's a large city. Stockford is small. If she got letters from him postmarked 'Stockford' she

might try to find him. Also, Betty knows there's another woman.
He wanted a divorce, remember? Then he tries to lull her. If
the other woman lives in Stockford, it wouldn't lull Betty very
much if his letters came from there. Furthermore, the other
woman probably knows nothing about Betty, in which case he's
not going to risk Betty's suddenly appearing on the scene."

"So now you figure his girlfriend lives in Stockford?"

"Probably right in Little Bohemia."

Wilks mulled that over for a moment. "Well, it makes some
sense," he admitted, "much as I hate to think of his being right
under our nose." He sat up again. "But what good's that going
to do us? Suppose you show his picture around and a dozen people say, 'Sure, that's good old Henry Smith only he left town
right after Labor Day and we don't have any forwarding address.' We're right where we've been all along, always too late."

"Except," Fellows said, "there's this other woman. If she's in
Little Bohemia, he might still be around."

"Bunk," Wilks said. "If he was still around, his Volkswagen
would be still around and we'd've picked it up. There isn't a place
in this county where a car could be hidden that we haven't
looked."

CHAPTER XXXII

Sunday, October 13, started off as just another routine day. Fellows held muster at quarter of eight, called the roll, carried out
inspection and read the duty list. He tacked the assignment sheet
on the bulletin board under Betty's smiling picture, did his
personal check of the log Daniels had kept and signed the
book.

Cassidy came in from his midnight to eight shift and the eight to four patrol went out. Fellows listened to an oral report of Cassidy's night, which had been an uneventful one, and sent him off for home and bed. He went into his office for a cup of coffee and wrote down a reminder to have Wilks go through the Stockford marriage licenses on Monday for Henry's name. If Henry actually had lived in Little Bohemia—and when his picture came in they'd find that out soon enough—he probably would not have left the place without his lady love. That might mean a Stockford marriage and it was worth looking into. And if it all turned out to be so, this would be the one time Henry wouldn't change his name when he moved. That would be too hard to explain to a new bride.

He contemplated the possibilities with carefully restrained hope then, since nothing could be done till the pictures came in, he put away his coffee and devoted his attention to the more current problems of the department.

At noon he took over the main desk while Unger went after more coffee for him and he ate a sandwich there in the lonely room. People were generally more law-abiding on the Sabbath and the place was quiet. No upset citizens came in, nobody phoned.

Unger returned and put the bag of coffee containers on the desk. "What's Wilks doing here on his day off?" he asked.

"I don't know," Fellows said, accepting the change and putting it in his pocket. "He outside?"

"Just drove in."

Fellows got out from behind the desk and let Unger resume the spot. Wilks opened the door and entered. "Heard anything?"

"Heard anything about what?"

"From Finney."

"Oh. No. Have some coffee?"

Unger told Wilks he was getting like the chief, coming in on his time off and Wilks said, "It's only because he doesn't give me enough to do." He took one of the containers and checked that it had milk and sugar. "All right, I'll drink it," he said. "Why do you suppose Finney hasn't called?"

"I don't know. I hadn't thought about it."

"Don't you think you ought to?"

"He'll call when he's got something to call about and when I hear from him I'll call you."

Wilks finished the coffee and said he was en route to pick up a newspaper. "Maybe I'll stop by on the way back."

The phone rang as he was going out the door and he paused to watch Unger answer. Unger motioned to the chief who said he'd take it in the office. He nodded at Wilks and put his hand over the mouthpiece. "New York," he said. Wilks acknowledged and followed the chief.

Finney was on the line and when Fellows got settled in his chair and lifted his receiver, the New York detective said, "I talked to Peggy Williams, Chief, but, gee, I'm afraid I messed it up."

"Yeah?" Fellows said. "How?"

"Well, I asked about her sister and did she ever hear from her and she said she did but not often. She said she'd kept the return addresses and I got a list of them. You want me to read them?"

"You bet I do." Fellows pulled over a pad and pencil.

Finney read them off. They were all "care ofs"; c/o Mosely in Schenectady; c/o Benton in Harrisburg; c/o Moore in Springfield, Ohio; and c/o Cooper at the Glenwood Road address. "She said," Finney went on, "that she got other letters without return addresses."

"So far so good. What else?"

"Well, what happened was I was asking her about writing to her sister and she said she didn't. I asked about how she ran into Henry and she told me about that. She never got to meet the girl. They were at a different table and when Henry saw her he came over to her table and talked. He didn't bring the girl over and he didn't introduce her."

"What'd the girl look like?"

"A very attractive blonde, Peggy—Miss Williams—said. Well dressed. Young. She seemed to have money."

"That's about what I figured. Go ahead."

"Well, Miss Williams told me Henry came hurrying over and he was all eager to explain that it was a business venture and that Betty had begged off from coming along because business deals bored her. I asked her if she believed him and she said, quick on the comeback, 'Would you?' She's a pretty smart girl, you know. A really attractive—well, anyway, I really goofed, I guess. I asked her if she was going to write Betty and tell her about this girl and she said no, it was none of her business. Then she explained to me that she and her sister had never been close. She said Betty had been too much the 'mother' in the household and she was near enough to Betty's age to resent it. She also said she resented Betty's running off and getting married, leaving her in charge of the boys when she was only fourteen. I have to say in all fairness to Miss Williams that she was very quick and honest and admitted that her resentment wasn't justified. She volunteered that herself."

"Yes, yes," Fellows said. "And she didn't write Betty back?"

"She said not more than two or three times. I think you have to understand her point of view."

Fellows said, "I think you're understanding it very well. What's this goof you're talking about?"

"Well," he said, chagrin in his tone, "from the way she talked, I mean about her and Betty not being close, I sort of figured it was O.K. to tell her what happened, I mean especially after she wanted to know what I was asking so many questions about her for. So I told her right out that Betty was dead. I guess I wasn't very tactful. If I'd only known—but she'd said—and I wasn't considerate. It was all my fault. I told her and she went all to pieces. I mean I couldn't do anything for her. I never dreamed she'd take it like that after what she said. I felt so helpless. I wouldn't have hurt her for anything. It was awful to see her cry like that."

"You couldn't have known," Fellows said gently.

"Yes, but I'm afraid I won't be able to talk to her any more for a day or two."

"You've covered it all already, haven't you? What didn't you ask her?"

"Well, I asked what you wanted me to but, well, I think I should go back. When she's feeling better."

"That," Fellows said, smiling, "is up to you. Tell me, though. Did Peggy think she could recognize this blonde girl again?"

"She's sure she could."

"She remember what she was wearing?"

"Yes, she did. She remembered everything about the girl very well. She said she was sure the whole thing was phony and something was going on because the blonde girl was not only with Henry but she was sporting a big diamond engagement ring!"

Fellows let out a whoop. "Thanks, Finney," he said. "Listen, I'll call you back." He slammed down the phone in front of a surprised Wilks and clapped his forehead. "That's it," he exclaimed. "How dumb can you get? The picture! I knew I'd seen him!"

Wilks stared at him. "Henry?"

Fellows dug for the case file among his papers. "We don't have to wait to go through the Stockford marriage records and we don't have to show his picture. I know who it is and I should have known yesterday just as soon as I figured he lived in Little Bohemia. The blonde girlfriend, the diamond ring. His name was Henry, even! I don't know why I had to wait for Finney to mention the ring before it came to me."

"You know who it is?"

"Yes. I forget his name but I've got it here." He found the file and opened it. "I thought the picture was familiar but when you said it wasn't anybody connected with the case I forgot about it. He *is* connected only you weren't around when he came in. Here it is. Hank Wilson. Savannah House on Number Four Street. One small block from Mrs. Fremont's. He was engaged to that Adele Edmunds who reported the Flashlight Kid. She said they were dancing at the pavilion at the time of the murder but that's a lie. She's covering for him."

"You're sure it's the same man?"

"You're damned right I'm sure. He's a lot older now than that glamorized high school portrait but there's a resemblance there all right and the rest fits him like a glove."

Wilks was skeptical. "You going to charge him on the basis of a resemblance to the picture?"

"That's what we'd be trying to do showing his picture around there. The only difference is *I'm* identifying it instead of somebody else."

"But he's got an alibi."

"And we're going to break it! Never mind your newspaper. We're going down to Little Bohemia."

CHAPTER XXXIII

The Savannah House on Number Four Street had a wide front porch and a weathered sign which creaked on its rod in the wind. The October day was cloudy and the brisk breeze harbored a taste of winter. All up and down the street the houses stared at each other coldly and they wore a naked, past-the-season look. People still lived in Little Bohemia but they were the year-round residents who nestled by their fires. The boisterous gaiety, the slacks and shorts of summer were gone.

Fellows and Wilks, coming into the unshuttered loneliness, parked their car on the sidewalk and crossed the stiff, noisy boards of the Savannah House porch to twist an old bellknob that clanged on the other side of the door.

The woman who let them in was thin and sharp-nosed. She wore steel-framed glasses and her face was pinched, as if by frost, her eyes as bleak as the clouded day. She bade them enter quickly and latched the door against the weather before she asked their business. "It costs like crazy to heat this old barn," she said. "I don't aim to heat the outdoors too."

It was cheerier in the hall for it was warm and comfortable

and the furnishings were homey. The forbidding face the Savannah House showed to the world was quite different from the mellow atmosphere it saved for those who crossed the threshold. Inside, the woman's features seemed less forbidding as if she too had a face for the world and a face for the home.

Fellows made introductions and learned their hostess was Mrs. Thomas Prince. "We understand," he said, "that a Henry Wilson lives here."

She looked slightly surprised and for a moment the chief had the sinking fear that Henry had given them still another false address. Then she said, "Why, not any more."

The policemen looked at each other, their faces falling slightly. Once more they were too late. The phantom Henry Larkin kept a constant lead on them and it seemed as if, though they kept closing the gap, they were Achilles chasing his uncatchable tortoise. "When did he leave?" Fellows asked, tight-lipped.

This time the chips fell his way. "Two weeks ago yesterday," Mrs. Prince said promptly. "He moved his things over to Dr. Edmunds' house the day of the wedding."

Fellows' grim face relaxed a little under the glint of hope. "Then he married Adele Edmunds?"

"That's right. On September twenty-eighth." Mrs. Prince was smiling now and her face was as warm and pleasant as the house. "It was a lovely wedding, I might add. I was invited, you know. I was his landlady but they both regarded me as a friend."

"And he's now living with the Edmunds?"

"That's my understanding. She came over that morning and took him and his things to her house. I thought it wasn't right, their seeing each other on their wedding day before the ceremony. I told them that would bring them bad luck but they just laughed and said they didn't believe in such things."

"Excuse me," Fellows interrupted. "She took him and his things in her car? Didn't he have a car, a Volkswagen?"

"Oh, he sold that. Got rid of it the day before the wedding as a matter of fact. He wasn't going to need it and he met some young man in a bar and they got talking about cars and he ended up selling it to him. Went up to Pittsfield with the man the afternoon before the wedding to make the sale."

Wilks turned to Fellows. "Wouldn't you just know?" he said. "I'll bet he was in Motor Vehicles transferring the registration the very moment I was looking his up."

"He's been a lucky guy," Fellows agreed.

"Oh, he's very lucky," Mrs. Prince put in. "He couldn't have found a sweeter girl. And such a lovely family. Dr. Edmunds is very well-to-do, you know. They had the wedding in the Episcopal Church in town and you never saw it so decorated. Then there was a reception at the Edmunds' afterwards. It was such a lovely affair and the Edmunds have such a beautiful house. You could put it up on Cobblers Lane and it would fit right in."

Fellows said, "Well, I guess that's the place to go to find him. By the way, how long had he been living here?"

"Since the middle of July. He came, I believe, on the fifteenth."

She paused and eyed the two men with the beginnings of suspicion. "Do you want him for something?"

Fellows nodded abruptly. "You remember the murder that took place on the beach on the night of August thirty-first, a Saturday night?"

"Oh my, but of course. Do you mean you want him in connection with that? He told you about the boy with the flashlight. I remember reading it in the paper. He said he thought it was foolish to mention it but Adele had insisted."

"Yes," Fellows said. "But it wasn't quite as foolish as he thought. We want to talk to him about it some more." He put on his casual air. "Incidentally, do you remember what he did that night?"

"Oh yes," Mrs. Prince said readily. "He was out with Adele. They went dancing at the pavilion."

"This is what he told you?"

"Yes."

"What time did they go?"

"He left here about nine o'clock to pick her up."

"Nine o'clock? He went out at nine o'clock and told you he was going to see Adele?"

"That's who he did see."

"You mean you *presume* that's who he saw."

Mrs. Prince wet her lips. "I don't presume anything of the kind. That's who he saw. Adele told me that herself."

Fellows said to Wilks, "She's backing him up all the way through. She must know what it's all about."

"What what's all about?" Mrs. Prince said sharply.

"What went on that night. They may both have told you they went to the pavilion but we don't think that's where they did go."

"They did so," she answered flatly. "I ought to know because I saw them there myself. So don't tell me where they went."

Both Fellows and Wilks blinked. "You saw them?"

"I went over myself that evening. I went over around ten o'clock and there they were, dancing together. Not only that but they treated me to a soda. And Henry danced with me."

Fellows was visibly shaken. "How long were you there?" he asked, fumbling.

"An hour, maybe longer."

"That tears it," Wilks said. "Now he's got a double alibi."

"Are you sure it was that night?" Fellows asked, still trying.

"Absolutely. Saturday night."

Wilks nudged the chief. "Come on, Sherlock. You got the picture wrong. Let's go. We're wasting time here."

Fellows shook him off. "One more thing, Mrs. Prince, if you please. May I see a sample of Henry Wilson's handwriting?"

"Handwriting? I don't know's I have any."

"He signed your register, didn't he?"

"That's right. I don't know what you think that's going to do."

"Could I see it, please?"

"Yes, if you want. You'll have to wait. I'll get it."

She went off and Wilks said, "Be sensible, Fred. You've got the wrong man. He was in the pavilion when the girl was killed."

"He's a con artist, Sid."

"He's not going to con Adele and this woman into alibiing him for murder, Fred. It's their necks too."

"It's not going to hurt anything to take a look at his handwriting."

"Adele, yes, if she was in it with him, but what's Mrs. Prince got to gain? And if Adele was in it, what would they show up at police headquarters for?"

Mrs. Prince came back with the ledger book. "Here's his signature," she said, as one going through an unpleasant duty. "And here's what he wrote when he left." She reread it herself and melted a little. "That's a sweet sentiment, don't you think? They were a dear couple and they felt like I was a real friend."

For answer, Fellows opened his notebook and took out the 'Peggy' letter. He spread it against the ledger Mrs. Prince still held while Wilks looked over her other shoulder. "What about that, Sid," he said with cold bitterness. "That's the same handwriting and no question. We're not the ones who're wrong. Not this time. Take a look, Mrs. Prince. Don't you agree that's the same handwriting?"

She said uneasily, "What's that letter?"

"It's a letter Henry Wilson wrote to his wife." Fellows straightened and turned on her. "Or maybe Mr. Wilson didn't tell you he had a wife. Or maybe he *did* tell you. Maybe he also told you his wife was the young girl who was murdered on the beach that Saturday night when you claim you saw him and Adele dancing in the pavilion!"

Mrs. Prince dropped the book and recoiled against the hall table, knocking over a figurine. "You're joking."

"No I'm not joking," he said relentlessly. "And you'd better not joke with me. Did you know that the murdered girl was Henry Wilson's wife?"

"No," she said, stunned and ashen. "No. I don't believe it."

"Do you want to read the letter he wrote her, that you can see for yourself is in his handwriting? Do you want to read how he ran into her sister while he was out with Adele? Do you want to read about the deal he was cooking up with Adele? Do you know what that deal was, Mrs. Prince? It was murder. It was the murder of his wife. That's what he and Adele were planning. That's how they managed it so they could have that beautiful wedding in the Episcopal Church two weeks ago. They murdered his former wife!"

"No," she shrieked and clapped her hands over her ears. "You're lying, you're lying." She reeled and Fellows caught her elbow. "I feel faint," she whispered.

The chief led her into the parlor and helped her to the couch. She slumped onto it, pasty-faced and staring. Fellows leaned over her. "And if you say you saw them dancing at the pavilion and they weren't dancing at the pavilion, that makes you an accomplice. That means you're in it with them."

She looked up and swallowed. "You've made a mistake. It couldn't be the way you say."

"It could and it is. That dear couple you love so much conspired to kill a sweet young girl because she stood in their way, because she wouldn't give Henry a divorce."

He went and pulled a chair close and sat down, taking a friendlier tone. "Don't try to protect them, Mrs. Prince. You don't want to get mixed up with a pair of murderers, do you? Now think carefully, Mrs. Prince. Did you go to the pavilion that Saturday night?"

"Maybe it was another Saturday night," she said nervously.

"Give me a straight answer, please. Did you see Henry and Adele at all that evening after Henry left the house at nine o'clock? I want the truth."

She nodded meekly. "Yes."

"At the pavilion?"

"No."

"Then it's only their sayso, isn't it, that they danced there?"

"Listen," she said pleadingly. "Please listen. If this is true, if that girl was Hank's wife, Adele doesn't know anything about it."

"I'm afraid she does, Mrs. Prince. She supported his alibi. She said they were dancing in the pavilion when the girl was killed."

"No she didn't. I made that up. She never said that at all."

"She said it to us, Mrs. Prince. She told us, the police, that that's what they were doing."

"But she didn't know," Mrs. Prince said. "She couldn't have known. Please. Let me tell you."

"By all means. Sid, get my notebook, will you? I dropped it in the hall."

Wilks had already collected the fallen items and he handed it to Fellows.

Mrs. Prince took a breath. "It started," she said in a hoarse whisper, "with Hank telling me he was going out with Adele. He went out at nine o'clock and told me he was going to see her which was quite natural because they were engaged. I expected they went dancing. So then, what happened was at about quarter of eleven who should ring the doorbell but Adele herself. I was surprised and I was even more surprised when it turned out she wanted to know if Hank was back home yet. It sounded like she hadn't seen him at all. I didn't know what it was all about except she was all excited and very anxious to see him.

"I had her come in and fixed us both some tea in the parlor and we talked and she told me she wasn't supposed to come here that evening because Hank was going to phone her but she couldn't wait any longer and thought maybe he wasn't going to call till tomorrow and she wanted to hear from him tonight. She wouldn't tell me why, though.

"We had the tea and we waited and finally Adele said I shouldn't stay up but she would because she couldn't sleep without knowing what had happened. I wouldn't hear of leaving her alone, though, and besides I was very curious about all this. After all, Hank was as straight and honest as any man and he would only tell me a deliberate falsehood in the direst extremity.

"Finally, about half past eleven in he came and he was very startled to find Adele. He said, very angrily, 'What are you doing here? You weren't supposed to come.' It was the only time I ever saw him lose his temper. It was only for a moment though. Adele was so apologetic and who could stay angry at Adele? She said she knew she wasn't supposed to come but she just couldn't wait and she didn't see what harm it could do. Then he said it did a lot of harm because he'd told me he was going to be out with her and now he was going to have to tell me what it was all about and it was supposed to be ultra-secret.

"They made me promise I'd never give it away that they weren't together that night and I swore I wouldn't and I wouldn't have told you a thing about it if—if—except that I can't let you think Adele is mixed up in the murder of that girl. And you're mistaken about Henry too. He was involved in a very very secret business meeting with some people and if it ever got out that he'd met with them, something awful would happen to the stock market. He said it might even cause another depression."

Fellows stared at her, open-mouthed. "He said *that*?"

She looked up and nodded at him, tight-faced. "All right, you got it out of me and maybe you're one of *them* who's trying to find out about that meeting but all I can say is you're going to be too late because the meeting was held over a month ago and they've done what they were going to do. And you go see Henry and he'll get the people he was with to protect him. He wasn't with Adele that night. He was with those other people." She swallowed and her eyes filled with tears. She put her hands over her face and said, "Oh, Hank, I didn't mean to tell. They just frightened me so!"

Fellows got slowly to his feet, shaking his head in wonder. He smiled sympathetically at the woman. "Don't you worry, Mrs. Prince," he said in a not unkind tone. "Your talking to us is not going to create a world-wide depression. Henry's important in his way but he's not that important."

He thanked her with an awkward pat on the shoulder, raised his eyebrows at Wilks and walked out.

CHAPTER XXXIV

Dr. Kyle Edmunds, well-to-do surgeon attached to the Stockford hospital, was out in an old sweater and worn khaki pants raking leaves when the chief and Wilks pulled up in front of his large, three-storied home. When the policemen got out of the car, Edmunds noted the uniform and strolled over, dragging the rake behind. He was a moderately tall, heavyset man with a ruddy face and gray, windswept hair. "You must be Fred Fellows," he said, observing the gold badge. "Anything I can do for you?"

"A few things, Dr. Edmunds, perhaps. This is Detective Sergeant Wilks."

They shook hands, Edmunds switching the rake. "You got a criminal who needs a bullet removed?" the doctor asked with an attempt at humor but his smile faded when neither officer reacted and his own face sobered. Apparently the business at hand was more serious than he'd thought. "Would you care to come in the house?" he asked then. "I presume it's me you want to see."

"Well no," Fellows said. "We would like to talk to your son-in-law if he's around."

Edmunds tried again. "What's he been up to, drunk driving, hit and run, embezzlement?"

Fellows made an attempt to be light-hearted himself. "No, none of those things. At least that we know about so far."

"Well, I'm afraid you'll just have to wait. My son-in-law and my daughter are away on their honeymoon. I guess you saw in the paper they got married two weeks ago."

"I've heard about it. When do you expect them back?"

"As a matter of fact we're picking them up at the airport in

Pittsfield at five o'clock." He looked at his watch. "They should be landing in New York any minute now. They've been to Bermuda, you know. Or maybe you don't know."

"No," Fellows said. "I didn't know. Well, since he's not here, I guess we will accept your invitation and go inside."

"My," said Edmunds, still smiling. "This really does sound serious."

Fellows didn't attempt to be light-hearted now. "Yes," he said. "Very serious."

Edmunds said no more till he let them into the front hallway of the house. "My wife is sleeping," he told them then, a vague concern in his face. "I don't know where the other children are. Come into the living room."

The room was large and pleasant with a feeling of whiteness about it though there was plenty of color. "Sit down," he said, gesturing at chairs while he stationed himself in front of a white trimmed brick fireplace. "Now what's this about?"

Fellows perched on the edge of a chair and planted his elbows on his knees. "It's hard having to talk to you about this sort of thing," he said. "Do you know much about your son-in-law—his background, I mean?"

"Yes. Of course I do. Why do you ask?"

"His qualifications for marriage to your daughter were suitable?"

Edmunds scowled pointedly. "I don't quite like the tone of this conversation. What do you mean were his qualifications suitable? Of course they were."

"You've met his family?"

"No. That would hardly be possible. He has none. His father died in 1957 and his mother died shortly after he graduated from Princeton."

"Oh?" Fellows said. "He went to Princeton?"

"Yes, he went to Princeton. Do you find that strange?"

"A little. I talked to his mother yesterday afternoon—and not in any seance, I might add—and I understand from her that he never went beyond high school."

"I think you're making a mistake," Edmunds said tightly. "You've got my son-in-law confused with somebody else."

"I wish that were the case, Dr. Edmunds, but I'm afraid it's not. His name is Henry Larkin, not Wilson, and he grew up in a poor section of the Bronx. He went through high school there and—"

"I'm telling you you've got the wrong man," Edmunds snapped. "I know my son-in-law. He was born and raised in southern New Jersey, the son of Henry Wilson, a well-known banker and a distant cousin of Woodrow Wilson. He entered Princeton in 1955 and graduated in 1959, cum laude. His father died in his sophomore year and it was found, unfortunately, that the father had overextended himself in his investments and Henry had to work his way through the last two years. Then his mother died and he was left with a little bit of money and nothing else."

Fellows said, "Have you seen his diploma from Princeton?"

"Come, man, be sensible. What fool goes around waving his diploma? All you have to do is talk to him to find out he knows Princeton."

"I'm sure he does. He lived around Princeton for a time, according to Mrs. Larkin."

Edmunds shook his head irritably. "You're still not convinced? I don't understand you."

"Have you checked into his background at all? All you're telling me is what he told you. That doesn't prove anything."

"Of course I haven't checked into his background. What do you think I do, put private detectives on every boy who comes around my girls? When a boy comes around, I meet that boy and I size that boy up and I can size a man up pretty well, let me tell you. If he's honest, I can tell it just as surely as I can tell if he's dishonest. And if he's honest you don't question his word. You don't have to. And Henry is a hard-working, ambitious, honest and intelligent young man. If he'd been anything else, I would have done everything in my power to dissuade my daughter from going through with the marriage. In the case of my son-in-law, nothing was farther from my mind. This is a boy who's going to go places and do things. He's got his feet on the ground and he's got what it takes. One of the things he's got is integrity. He doesn't have to tell me about his background and he doesn't have to prove to me he's who he says he is. All I need to do is see the man himself and I can tell the rest."

"Do you know where he was living while he was courting your daughter?"

"Yes. Little Bohemia I believe it's called. I suppose you're going to try to tell me he lived somewhere else."

"No, that's the place all right, though it strikes me as a strange place for a young man on his way up."

"You really are hard-headed, aren't you?" Edmunds said. "Did you really think I'd be upset at this disclosure? If you had found out as much about him as I have, you'd know that he was an art major in college and that it was his ambition to paint. He moved to Little Bohemia to indulge this fancy of his while living off the tiny income from his inheritance. But he was wise enough and smart enough to know that this was something he could only do while he was single. As he said to me, it was not his intention to make any woman play second-fiddle to a canvas and as he knew he could never become a great artist he was content to have gotten it out of his system. Now that he wanted to marry he was changing his sights, putting painting aside and going into business."

"Is he in business?" Fellows asked.

"As of the moment he does not have a position, no. But with his contacts and his father's friends there's no trouble there. In fact, a very big position in the banking field is all but set for him."

"Who paid for this honeymoon to Bermuda?" Fellows asked bluntly.

Edmunds' chin went up. "He did, of course."

"I thought he had very little money."

"He has enough for that. When they come back, of course, they'll live with us until his position comes through."

"Can you tell me what this position is, Dr. Edmunds?"

"I don't know exactly except that it's in the banking field and has to do with his late father in some way. It was pretty complicated the way he explained it."

"I'll bet it was."

"I don't like the tone of your voice, Chief. I'm a doctor, not a banker and I know nothing of high finance."

"Was it about this position that he had an important meeting the night of the murder?"

"Murder? What murder?"

"The girl who was found on the beach. The Saturday just before Labor Day. That seems a strange night to have an important meeting."

"It was a secret meeting and that is, no doubt, why it was held on a strange night. I don't understand how you heard anything about it."

Fellows' mouth twisted. "I'm curious, Dr. Edmunds. This was a very secret meeting I understand. All sorts of calamities would happen if the word got out. What on earth can a twenty-six year old boy have that makes it so vital that his presence at a meeting be kept secret?"

Edmunds had an answer to that one. "His father's name! I understood that much. It's some kind of reorganization that would have wide repercussions if it were known that a *Wilson* was going to be in it. It was a business coup and Henry stands to make a great deal of money the moment it goes through but it wouldn't stand a chance if the word got out."

"And did he make a lot of money?"

"It hasn't been settled yet, whatever it is."

"And his father is supposed to be a famous banker? I don't believe I know the name. Had you heard of him before you met Henry?"

"Of course not. As I told you, I know nothing about banking."

"Which was probably why Henry chose the field," Fellows said.

Edmunds snapped back at that one. "You seem determined to believe he's some sort of impostor. You're absolutely out of your mind. Good heavens, man, do you think for a moment a fraud would represent himself as the son of a famous banker,

a kin to a former president of the United States and the graduate
of a well-known university if none of these things were true?
Why this could be checked so fast he'd be revealed in no time."

Fellows said, "But you didn't check, did you, Doctor? The
bolder his credentials the more you accept them on face value.
I don't like to have to tell you this, sir, but I'm very much afraid
your son-in-law is a fraud and a good deal more. Did you know,
for example, that he had a wife before he married Adele?"

"He had a wife? I don't believe it. Where is she?"

"She's dead, Dr. Edmunds. She's the girl who was found
strangled on the beach at Little Bohemia."

Edmunds sank back against the fireplace and his ruddy com-
plexion drained white. "That girl," he said in a faint voice,
"was Henry's wife?" He rallied himself a little. "I don't believe it."

"He wanted a divorce from her after he met Adele," Fellows
went on. "She wouldn't give it to him."

Edmunds was gray. He pointed a shaking finger at the chief.
"You're insinuating that he did away with her. You're trying to
say my son-in-law murdered that woman."

"That's the way it looks, Dr. Edmunds. I'm sorry."

Edmunds shook his head. "No. You're out of your mind. I
know my son-in-law and I know he's utterly incapable of such
a thing. It's conceivable that he might misrepresent. I don't believe it but it's conceivable. But to commit murder? You'll
never get me to believe a thing like that."

Fellows said, "I know these things are hard to accept sometimes. Can you tell us what he did on the night of the murder?
I don't mean what he *told* you he did but what you saw him
do?"

Edmunds shook his head numbly. "I don't know that I
can. He and Adele were around here in the afternoon and then
he left immediately after an early supper to go home and change
for the meeting."

"You mean he left. You don't really know where he went.
What time was that?"

"Around seven."

"And Adele?"

"She waited to hear what happened at the meeting. She was around here all evening on pins and needles waiting for him to phone. A great deal of money was involved and if things worked out as he hoped he'd be a wealthy young man. We were all in a good deal of suspense about that."

"Adele left the house later in the evening, didn't she?"

"Yes. Around ten thirty. She couldn't stand the suspense any more. She said she was going to his place. I suppose I can't swear that's where she *did* go but that's where she told me she was going."

"When did you see her next?"

"Not till the next morning. I don't know what time she got in. Henry never did call here but she told me that there were complications at the meeting. Something about the SEC having to approve and it would take time."

"And as of right now Henry still has no money?"

"That's all right. He's welcome to share with us. If this deal falls through he won't have to worry. He'll make it. No question about that. And I'll be glad to stake him until he does." Edmunds' color and some of his fire was returning. "You've gone off the track somewhere. You've got onto the wrong man."

Fellows didn't argue the point. He said, "Henry's already moved his things in here, I believe. Since you're so convinced of his innocence would you be willing to let us look through them?"

Edmunds pondered for a moment. "Yes," he said, his voice coming up. "I don't have the right to go through another person's belongings but, under the circumstances, I'll take the responsibility and settle the question."

He led the two men up the stairs and down a hall to the back. A bedroom door opened and Mrs. Edmunds appeared. She was a frail, petite woman but one with strength and resiliency. Edmunds paused to introduce the policemen and said, "They've got the most fantastic story you ever heard, Viola. It would be comical if it weren't so serious. They're trying to say Henry was mixed up with the girl who was murdered on the beach. Not just mixed up with her but married to her."

Mrs. Edmunds said, "Ridiculous. They should know better."

"That's what I've been trying to tell them. I'm going to let them look at Henry's things. It's silly but it may get them untracked."

"I don't approve, but never argue with the police. They're never wrong."

She went the other way and Edmunds showed Fellows and Wilks into a large airy bedroom overlooking the leaf-covered yard and empty swimming pool at the rear. He threw open a closet door to reveal several suits of clothes and said, "The maid unpacked his things. It's all here except what he took to Bermuda. This is his bureau. That one's Adele's and that closet's hers. You can look through those too if you want but I'm going to watch what you do and I'm going to insist that you replace everything as you found it."

Fellows assured him they'd be careful and they started through the dresser and the closet. The clothes they explored were well made and of good quality, even better than Betty's had been. They went with a Princeton graduate, though one with more money than Henry was supposed to have had.

As for clues, however, there were none. There was not so much as a scrap of handwriting to compare with the "Peggy" letter or a photograph to match with Mrs. Larkin's picture of a seventeen year old boy.

"Satisfied?" Edmunds said with a trace of contempt when the two men replaced the last object and closed the final drawer.

Fellows was anything but satisfied. He well knew he had no case, that his only evidence was a supposed similarity of penmanship, noted only by his inexpert eye, and the apparent resemblance of a man he'd seen briefly and scarcely remembered to a picture taken nine years before. He refused to back off, however, for that would leave him with nothing and, hiding his self-doubts he forged ahead, determined to see it through. "There's nothing here that means anything one way or the other," he replied. "You say their plane arrives at the airport in Pittsfield at five o'clock?"

Edmunds almost choked. "Now wait a minute. You don't think you're going to meet that plane!"

Wilks had his own misgivings but Fellows went on doggedly. "I was going to ask if we could go along with you. In our own car, of course. It might be easier that way."

"Easier than what?"

"It might make things easier if we were with you rather than on our own out there."

"Now listen," Edmunds said, his choler rising. "I'm not going to have you going to any airport. They've just had a honeymoon and I'm damned if I'm going to allow it to be spoiled by having a couple of policemen waiting for them at the steps of the plane. If you're still not convinced you've made a mistake you can come around and talk to Henry tomorrow. He'll be here. You don't have to worry about that."

Fellows' jaw was set. "I'm sorry, Dr. Edmunds, but we have our job to do."

"Your job can wait till tomorrow."

"My job, Doctor, is to talk to your son-in-law. I've been trying to do this for six weeks and now that I've got the chance I'm not going to risk losing it."

"You won't be losing anything. I guarantee you he's not going anywhere. I guarantee he'll be here any time you want to talk to him."

"I'm afraid that's something you aren't in a position to guarantee. We're going to be at that airport and we're going to pick him up when he gets off the plane. There'd be less fuss about it if we were with you but with you or without you we're going to be there."

Edmunds said bitterly, "If it's going to be like that then you'd better go with us. But you're going to regret spoiling a honeymoon couple's homecoming. That's one thing I *can* guarantee!"

CHAPTER XXXV

The plane was a propeller driven DC-3 doing the local run from New York to Boston with stops at Pittsfield and Springfield and it touched down at 5:03 P.M., taxiing around to the unloading gate. A dozen people were on hand to meet it and seven of the twelve were waiting for Mr. and Mrs. Henry Wilson. Four were family, Dr. and Mrs. Edmunds and their two younger daughters, and three were policemen, Fellows, Wilks and Pittsfield detective John Kelly.

Adele was first off, glowingly beautiful in a half-length mink and a mink hat and she stepped down quickly and ran into her mother's arms. Henry, looking dapper in an Ivy League topcoat came more slowly and he spotted the police in the group as Adele had not. His somber expression didn't change but he seemed still slower as he approached, ignoring them, to shake hands with Edmunds.

Adele kissed and hugged all around the family and Henry planted a dutiful kiss on his mother-in-law's cheek and shook hands with the younger girls. Then Edmunds said, "This is the chief of police," to Adele and she saw him at last. "Oh yes, I know. We've met." She smiled and shook his hand. "Hank, you remember Chief Fellows."

Henry allowed that he did and shook hands too. Adele said, "Whatever are you doing here?"

Edmunds picked up that question. "The chief has something to ask Henry which is too ridiculous to dignify with explanation." He turned. "Go ahead, Chief. This is what you wanted, isn't it?"

Fellows, however, wasn't looking at Henry. He reached out

and took Adele's wrist. "What a lovely watch, Mrs. Wilson,"
he said, pushing back her sleeve. "Look, Sid. Have you ever seen
such a beauty? One, two three—ten diamonds around the face.
Cut diamonds they are."

"Thank you," Adele said, beaming. "I'm just crazy about it."
She hugged her husband's arm with her free hand and gazed
up at his face. "Hank gave it to me for a wedding present."

THE PERENNIAL LIBRARY MYSTERY SERIES

E. C. Bentley

TRENT'S LAST CASE
"One of the three best detective stories ever written."
—Agatha Christie

TRENT'S OWN CASE
"I won't waste time saying that the plot is sound and the detection satisfying. Trent has not altered a scrap and reappears with all his old humor and charm."
—Dorothy L. Sayers

Gavin Black

A DRAGON FOR CHRISTMAS
"Potent excitement!"
—*New York Herald Tribune*

THE EYES AROUND ME
"I stayed up until all hours last night reading *The Eyes Around Me,* which is something I do not do very often, but I was so intrigued by the ingeniousness of Mr. Black's plotting and the witty way in which he spins his mystery. I can only say that I enjoyed the book enormously."
—F. van Wyck Mason

YOU WANT TO DIE, JOHNNY?
"Gavin Black doesn't just develop a pressure plot in suspense, he adds uninfected wit, character, charm, and sharp knowledge of the Far East to make rereading as keen as the first race-through."   —*Book Week*

Nicholas Blake

THE BEAST MUST DIE
"It remains one more proof that in the hands of a really first-class writer the detective novel can safely challenge comparison with any other variety of fiction."
—*The Manchester Guardian*

THE CORPSE IN THE SNOWMAN
"If there is a distinction between the novel and the detective story (which we do not admit), then this book deserves a high place in both categories."
—*The New York Times*

THE DREADFUL HOLLOW
"Pace unhurried, characters excellent, reasoning solid."
—*San Francisco Chronicle*

Nicholas Blake (cont'd)

THE WORM OF DEATH

"It [The Worm of Death] is one of Blake's very best—and his best is better than almost anyone's." —Louis Untermeyer

Christianna Brand

GREEN FOR DANGER

"You have to reach for the greatest of Great Names (Christie, Carr, Queen . . .) to find Brand's rivals in the devious subtleties of the trade."
—Anthony Boucher

Marjorie Carleton

VANISHED (*available 11/81*)

"Exceptional . . . a minor triumph."
—Jacques Barzun and Wendell Hertig Taylor, *A Catalogue of Crime*

George Harmon Coxe

MURDER WITH PICTURES

"[Coxe] has hit the bull's-eye with his first shot."
—*The New York Times*

Edmund Crispin

BURIED FOR PLEASURE

"Absolute and unalloyed delight."
—Anthony Boucher, *The New York Times*

D. M. Devine

MY BROTHER'S KILLER (*available 11/81*)

"A most enjoyable crime story which I enjoyed reading down to the last moment." —Agatha Christie

Kenneth Fearing

THE BIG CLOCK

"It will be some time before chill-hungry clients meet again so rare a compound of irony, satire, and icy-fingered narrative. *The Big Clock* is . . . a psychothriller you won't put down." —*Weekly Book Review*

Andrew Garve

THE ASHES OF LODA
"Garve . . . embellishes a fine fast adventure story with a more credible picture of the U.S.S.R. than is offered in most thrillers."

—The New York Times Book Review

THE CUCKOO LINE AFFAIR
". . . an agreeable and ingenious piece of work."   *—The New Yorker*

A HERO FOR LEANDA
"One can trust Mr. Garve to put a fresh twist to any situation, and the ending is really a lovely surprise."   *—The Manchester Guardian*

MURDER THROUGH THE LOOKING GLASS
". . . refreshingly out-of-the-way and enjoyable . . . highly recommended to all comers."   *—Saturday Review*

NO TEARS FOR HILDA
"It starts fine and finishes finer. I got behind on breathing watching Max get not only his man but his woman, too."   —Rex Stout

THE RIDDLE OF SAMSON
"The story is an excellent one, the people are quite likable, and the writing is superior."   *—Springfield Republican*

Michael Gilbert

BLOOD AND JUDGMENT
"Gilbert readers need scarcely be told that the characters all come alive at first sight, and that his surpassing talent for narration enhances any plot. . . . Don't miss."   *—San Francisco Chronicle*

THE BODY OF A GIRL
"Does what a good mystery should do: open up into all kinds of ramifications, with untold menace behind the action. At the end, there is a bang-up climax, and it is a pleasure to see how skilfully Gilbert wraps everything up."   *—The New York Times Book Review*

THE DANGER WITHIN
"Michael Gilbert has nicely combined some elements of the straight detective story with plenty of action, suspense, and adventure, to produce a superior thriller."   *—Saturday Review*

DEATH HAS DEEP ROOTS
"Trial scenes superb; prowl along Loire vivid chase stuff; funny in right places; a fine performance throughout."   *—Saturday Review*

Michael Gilbert (cont'd)

FEAR TO TREAD
"Merits serious consideration as a work of art."
—The New York Times

C. W. Grafton

BEYOND A REASONABLE DOUBT
"A very ingenious tale of murder . . . a brilliant and gripping narrative."
—Jacques Barzun and Wendell Hertig Taylor

Edward Grierson

THE SECOND MAN
"One of the best trial-testimony books to have come along in quite a while." *—The New Yorker*

Cyril Hare

DEATH IS NO SPORTSMAN *(available 12/81)*
"You will be thrilled because it succeeds in placing an ingenious story in a new and refreshing setting. . . . The identity of the murderer is really a surprise." *—Daily Mirror*

DEATH WALKS THE WOODS *(available 12/81)*
"Here is a fine formal detective story, with a technically brilliant solution demanding the attention of all connoisseurs of construction."
—Anthony Boucher, *The New York Times Book Review*

AN ENGLISH MURDER
"By a long shot, the best crime story I have read for a long time. Everything is traditional, but originality does not suffer. The setting is perfect. Full marks to Mr. Hare." *—Irish Press*

TRAGEDY AT LAW
"An extremely urbane and well-written detective story."
—The New York Times

UNTIMELY DEATH
"The English detective story at its quiet best, meticulously underplayed, rich in perceivings of the droll human animal and ready at the last with a neat surprise which has been there all the while had we but wits to see it." *—New York Herald Tribune Book Review*

Cyril Hare (cont'd)

WITH A BARE BODKIN
"One of the best detective stories published for a long time."
—*The Spectator*

Robert Harling

THE ENORMOUS SHADOW
"In some ways the best spy story of the modern period. . . . The writing is terse and vivid . . . the ending full of action . . . altogether first-rate."
—Jacques Barzun and Wendell Hertig Taylor, *A Catalogue of Crime*

Matthew Head

THE CABINDA AFFAIR
"An absorbing whodunit and a distinguished novel of atmosphere."
—Anthony Boucher, *The New York Times*

MURDER AT THE FLEA CLUB
"The true delight is in Head's style, its limpid ease combined with humor and an awesome precision of phrase."   —*San Francisco Chronicle*

M. V. Heberden

ENGAGED TO MURDER
"Smooth plotting."   —*The New York Times*

James Hilton

WAS IT MURDER?
"The story is well planned and well written."
—*The New York Times*

Elspeth Huxley

THE AFRICAN POISON MURDERS
"Obscure venom, manical mutilations, deadly bush fire, thrilling climax compose major opus.... Top-flight."
—*Saturday Review of Literature*

Francis Iles

BEFORE THE FACT
"Not many 'serious' novelists have produced character studies to compare with Iles's internally terrifying portrait of the murderer in *Before the Fact,* his masterpiece and a work truly deserving the appellation of unique and beyond price."   —Howard Haycraft

Francis Iles (cont'd)

MALICE AFORETHOUGHT
"It is a long time since I have read anything so good as *Malice Afore-thought,* with its cynical humour, acute criminology, plausible detail and rapid movement. It makes you hug yourself with pleasure."

—H. C. Harwood, *Saturday Review*

Lange Lewis

THE BIRTHDAY MURDER
"Almost perfect in its playlike purity and delightful prose."

—Jacques Barzun and Wendell Hertig Taylor

Arthur Maling

LUCKY DEVIL
"The plot unravels at a fast clip, the writing is breezy and Maling's approach is as fresh as today's stockmarket quotes."

—*Louisville Courier Journal*

RIPOFF
"A swiftly paced story of today's big business is larded with intrigue as a Ralph Nader-type investigates an insurance scandal and is soon on the run from a hired gun and his brother. . . . Engrossing and credible."

—*Booklist*

SCHROEDER'S GAME
"As the title indicates, this Schroeder is up to something, and the un-ravelling of his game is a diverting and sufficiently blood-soaked enter-tainment."

—*The New Yorker*

Thomas Sterling

THE EVIL OF THE DAY
"Prose as witty and subtle as it is sharp and clear. . .characters unconven-tionally conceived and richly bodied forth . . . . In short, a novel to be treasured."

—Anthony Boucher, *The New York Times*

Julian Symons

THE BELTING INHERITANCE
"A superb whodunit in the best tradition of the detective story."

—August Derleth, *Madison Capital Times*

Hillary Waugh

LAST SEEN WEARING . . .
"A brilliant tour de force."   —Julian Symons

THE MISSING MAN
"The quiet detailed police work of Chief Fred C. Fellows, Stockford, Conn., is at its best in *The Missing Man* . . . one of the Chief's toughest cases and one of the best handled."
                    —Anthony Boucher, *The New York Times Book Review*

Henry Kitchell Webster

WHO IS THE NEXT?
"A double murder, private-plane piloting, a neat impersonation, and a delicate courtship are adroitly combined by a writer who knows how to use the language."   —Jacques Barzun and Wendell Hertig Taylor

Anna Mary Wells

MURDERER'S CHOICE
"Good writing, ample action, and excellent character work."
                                      —*Saturday Review of Literature*

A TALENT FOR MURDER
"The discovery of the villain is a decided shock."   —*Books*

Edward Young

THE FIFTH PASSENGER
"Clever and adroit . . . excellent thriller"   —*Library Journal*

If you enjoyed this book you'll want to know about
THE PERENNIAL LIBRARY MYSTERY SERIES

Nicholas Blake

☐	P 456	THE BEAST MUST DIE	$1.95
☐	P 427	THE CORPSE IN THE SNOWMAN	$1.95
☐	P 493	THE DREADFUL HOLLOW	$1.95
☐	P 397	END OF CHAPTER	$1.95
☐	P 398	HEAD OF A TRAVELER	$2.25
☐	P 419	MINUTE FOR MURDER	$1.95
☐	P 520	THE MORNING AFTER DEATH	$1.95
☐	P 521	A PENKNIFE IN MY HEART	$2.25
☐	P 531	THE PRIVATE WOUND	$2.25
☐	P 494	A QUESTION OF PROOF	$1.95
☐	P 495	THE SAD VARIETY	$2.25
☐	P 428	THOU SHELL OF DEATH	$1.95
☐	P 418	THE WHISPER IN THE GLOOM	$1.95
☐	P 399	THE WIDOW'S CRUISE	$2.25
☐	P 400	THE WORM OF DEATH	$2.25

E. C. Bently

☐	P 440	TRENT'S LAST CASE	$2.50
☐	P 516	TRENT'S OWN CASE	$2.25

Buy them at your local bookstore or use this coupon for ordering:

HARPER & ROW, Mail Order Dept. #PMS, 10 East 53rd St., New York, N.Y. 10022.

Please send me the books I have checked above. I am enclosing $ _____ which includes a postage and handling charge of $1.00 for the first book and 25¢ for each additional book. Send check or money order. No cash or C.O.D.'s please.

Name _____

Address _____

City _____ State _____ Zip _____

Please allow 4 weeks for delivery. USA and Canada only. This offer expires 8/1/82 . Please add applicable sales tax.

Gavin Black

☐ P 473 A DRAGON FOR CHRISTMAS $1.95
☐ P 485 THE EYES AROUND ME $1.95
☐ P 472 YOU WANT TO DIE, JOHNNY? $1.95

Christianna Brand

☐ P 551 GREEN FOR DANGER $2.50

Marjorie Carleton

☐ P 559 VANISHED *(available 11/81)* $2.50

George Harmon Coxe

☐ P 527 MURDER WITH PICTURES $2.25

Edmund Crispin

☐ P 506 BURIED FOR PLEASURE $1.95

D. M. Devine

☐ P 558 MY BROTHER'S KILLER
         (available 11/81) $2.50

Kenneth Fearing

☐ P 500 THE BIG CLOCK $1.95

Buy them at your local bookstore or use this coupon for ordering:

**HARPER & ROW, Mail Order Dept. #PMS, 10 East 53rd St.,
New York, N.Y. 10022.**

Please send me the books I have checked above. I am enclosing $ _____
which includes a postage and handling charge of $1.00 for the first book and
25¢ for each additional book. Send check or money order. No cash or
C.O.D.'s please.

Name _____

Address _____

City _____ State _____ Zip _____

Please allow 4 weeks for delivery. USA and Canada only. This offer expires
8/1/82 . Please add applicable sales tax.

Andrew Garve

☐	P 430	THE ASHES OF LODA	$1.50
☐	P 451	THE CUCKOO LINE AFFAIR	$1.95
☐	P 429	A HERO FOR LEANDA	$1.50
☐	P 449	MURDER THROUGH THE LOOKING GLASS	$1.95
☐	P 441	NO TEARS FOR HILDA	$1.95
☐	P 450	THE RIDDLE OF SAMSON	$1.95

Michael Gilbert

☐	P 446	BLOOD AND JUDGMENT	$1.95
☐	P 459	THE BODY OF A GIRL	$1.95
☐	P 448	THE DANGER WITHIN	$1.95
☐	P 447	DEATH HAS DEEP ROOTS	$1.95
☐	P 458	FEAR TO TREAD	$1.95

C. W. Grafton

☐	P 519	BEYOND A REASONABLE DOUBT	$1.95

Edward Grierson

☐	P 528	THE SECOND MAN	$2.25

Buy them at your local bookstore or use this coupon for ordering:

HARPER & ROW, Mail Order Dept. #PMS, 10 East 53rd St., New York, N.Y. 10022.
Please send me the books I have checked above. I am enclosing $ _____ which includes a postage and handling charge of $1.00 for the first book and 25¢ for each additional book. Send check or money order. No cash or C.O.D.'s please.

Name _____

Address _____

City _____ State _____ Zip _____

Please allow 4 weeks for delivery. USA and Canada only. This offer expires 8/1/82. Please add applicable sales tax.

Cyril Hare

Buy them at your local bookstore or use this coupon for ordering:

Francis Iles

☐ P 517 BEFORE THE FACT $1.95
☐ P 532 MALICE AFORETHOUGHT $1.95

Lange Lewis

☐ P 518 THE BIRTHDAY MURDER $1.95

Arthur Maling

☐ P 482 LUCKY DEVIL $1.95
☐ P 483 RIPOFF $1.95
☐ P 484 SCHROEDER'S GAME $1.95

Austin Ripley

☐ P 387 MINUTE MYSTERIES $1.95

Thomas Sterling

☐ P 529 THE EVIL OF THE DAY $2.25

Julian Symons

☐ P 468 THE BELTING INHERITANCE $1.95
☐ P 469 BLAND BEGINNING $1.95
☐ P 481 BOGUE'S FORTUNE $1.95
☐ P 480 THE BROKEN PENNY $1.95
☐ P 461 THE COLOR OF MURDER $1.95
☐ P 460 THE 31ST OF FEBRUARY $1.95

Buy them at your local bookstore or use this coupon for ordering:

HARPER & ROW, Mail Order Dept. #PMS, 10 East 53rd St., New York, N.Y. 10022.

Please send me the books I have checked above. I am enclosing $ _____ which includes a postage and handling charge of $1.00 for the first book and 25¢ for each additional book. Send check or money order. No cash or C.O.D.'s please.

Name _____

Address _____

City _____ State _____ Zip _____

Please allow 4 weeks for delivery. USA and Canada only. This offer expires 8/1/82. Please add applicable sales tax.

Dorothy Stockbridge Tillet
(John Stephen Strange)

Buy them at your local bookstore or use this coupon for ordering:

HARPER & ROW, Mail Order Dept. #PMS, 10 East 53rd St., New York, N.Y. 10022.

Please send me the books I have checked above. I am enclosing $ _____ which includes a postage and handling charge of $1.00 for the first book and 25¢ for each additional book. Send check or money order. No cash or C.O.D.'s please.

Name _____

Address _____

City _____ State _____ Zip _____

Please allow 4 weeks for delivery. USA and Canada only. This offer expires 8/1/82. Please add applicable sales tax.